Louise

CW00727422

THE SIEGE OF
BABYLON

Silver Book Box
Series editor: Julia Eccleshare

SILVER BOOK BOX

THE SIEGE OF BABYLON

Farrukh Dhondy

MACMILLAN

First published by Macmillan 1978
First published in *Silver Book Box* 1989

Published by
MACMILLAN EDUCATION LTD
Houndmills, Basingstoke, Hampshire RG21 2XS
and London
Companies and representatives
throughout the world

Series designer Julian Holland

Cover illustration Tony Gibbons

Printed in Hong Kong

British Library Cataloguing in Publication Data
Dhondy, Farrukh, 1944-
The siege of Babylon.
I. Title II. Series
823[F]
ISBN 0–333–47179–2

For the *Race Today* Collective

One

Hurly stands behind the half-drawn curtain so that he can look into the street but can't be seen from it. The police have mounted three huge searchlights on tripods, and they light up the ground outside with the artificial daylight of a football field. The glare from two of them is directly in Hurly's eyes. The third is out of sight, mounted outside one of the adjoining buildings. If he pushes his head back, right up against the frame of the window, he can see wire barriers that have been thrown up thirty yards down the street. Beyond the encircling barriers, just outside the circle of light, he can sense the presence of an unnumbered crowd. Their audience. Now and again he fancies that the flash of a camera has burst above the heads of those people, but he can't be sure; it may be some other kind of flare.

Within the circle of light nobody moves. At the edge of the circle, just under the window out of which he is looking, Hurly can see a blue-uniformed policeman standing casually, his arms behind his back, his head perpetually sideways like the face on a coin. Below his blue starred helmet the clean-cut features are unrecognisable.

'Bully still stand up out there?' Hurly hears Kwate's voice behind him.

'Can't see nothing. They've place a man under here.'

Hurly has been at the window for hours. 'I tired of looking,' he says.

He draws his body into the shelter of the wall and glances at Kwate who is sitting with his back straight, his head tilted and resting, looking cool and collected on a chair in the centre of the room. Beyond him, between the door to the corridor and the door to the kitchen, Rupert has drawn up a stool. Against the mantelpiece, next to the tattered divan, their faces to the wall, their backs bent like question marks, arms raised and palms spread flat, resting, their weight shifting from haunch to haunch on the three-legged stools, sit their four hostages.

From time to time the Greek man with the face like the fiddler on the roof and a droopy moustache, turns around and tries to plead with Kwate.

'I am poor man, working hard. You is like my son. We come on your side now, we come on your side.'

Kwate's forearm is outstretched, steady. In his hand, pointing at the two men and at the young boy and the girl, is the Smith and Wesson automatic. On Rupert's spread thighs rests the shotgun.

Hurly transfers the Browning from his left to his right hand and wipes the sweat off its butt. He is not sure where to point it, so he holds it drooping down by his side.

'They go cut the electricity,' he says.

'How do you know?'

'They've brought up a whole heap of searchlight and thing outside.'

'I want sight it,' Kwate says, and rising from the chair, backs slowly, cautiously, to change places with Hurly. Hurly gets to the chair and imitates Kwate's sitting position. Once again there is silence in the room.

They seem to be waiting for Kwate. Hurly can now hear the breath of the big man, regular as a clock. Occasionally a stool creaks as the weight of a weary body shifts on it. The noise of traffic comes in through the window behind the hum of some machine that has begun throbbing in the street below.

'I goin' call out,' Kwate says, casually, as though announcing to the others that he is going for a leak.

Hurly's eyes dart towards him and then back to the watchers at the wall.

'Burgess!' Kwate shouts, and then again, stretching the two syllables, 'Bur—gess!'

Hurly can hear the buzz of the crowd outside. The sound seems to come through the still air. They have heard Kwate's shout. Then there is the voice on a loud-hailer telling the people to get away from the railings.

There is a stamp of boots and a voice, tinny but amplified through the hailer, calls back, 'We're still here.'

Kwate doesn't reply.

Then the voice again:

'Kwate.'

The name rings out like a clap in an empty courtyard. Hurly sees Kwate's eyes leap to the hostages to see if the sound of his name has any effect on them. The police haven't used any names before. As Kwate raised the double-glazed window when the police moved in, Chief Superintendent Burgess introduced himself to them.

Now they know our names, Hurly thinks, and it makes him feel that somehow the police are getting closer. He backs towards the kitchen door.

'Stop your dancing,' Kwate says. 'Snipers. Babylon will mount snipers in them room across the street. Keep down if you want to come out of here *on* your feet instead of *after* them.'

9

'They wouldn't shoot; they might get one of these lot,' Hurly says.

'No, boy, them snipers trained. They could make out a black face from a whitey nose from three thousand yards.'

'They would shoot us, them, anybody,' Rupert says, more to the prisoners than to Kwate.

Hurly watches the hostages carefully. All through the night he has watched them, admitting to himself that he is afraid, actually frightened of these four helpless people they are holding.

'Kwate,' Burgess calls out again.

How do they know his name? Hurly thinks. If they got it out of police records, it wouldn't say *Kwate*, it would say: *Aloysius Brown, b. 1948, Kingston, Jamaica. Colour of eyes: dark brown, negroid hair. Identifying marks: scar on left side of neck. Three years juvenile detention, nine months for causing actual bodily harm. Involved with black extremist political groups.*

They'd been picked up, Hurly remembers, one night walking home from a blues party.

'Your name?' the sergeant on duty at Kennington police station asked.

'Kwate.'

Slap. He hit Kwate with the heel of his palm straight in the face. 'I want your name, Sunshine, not your boogey-boogey.'

'Aloysius Brown.'

'That's more like it.'

'Kwate, you can't hope to gain anything.' Burgess's voice is eerily clear. 'Have you thought it over? You don't have much time.'

'Don't cut the light.' Kwate shouts back. His voice echoes round the room.

'Say that again?'

'Don't mess with the electricity. If you blow the light we gonna blast one of them hostages and throw them out the window at you.'

For a few moments there is silence outside the window, then the sound of voices consulting.

'We have no intention of cutting off the electricity. Our men can see all of you in the room. Do you want to co-operate with us and tell us your names?'

'Rest it,' Kwate says, and sliding along the wall he thumbs off the light switch.

'What are you doing?' Hurly asks. The darkness is soft to his eyes at first, but soon he begins to pick out the shapes he is guarding. The kitchen light is still on and throws long shadows in the room.

The girl breaks the silence. 'I can't sit like this any more.'

'Shut your mouth, woman,' Kwate snaps.

'I really can't. My arms ache. I feel itchy.'

'Hold them where we could see them. You ought to have more bath, filthy bitch.'

'Where does it itch?' Rupert asks.

'Don't talk to them, man, this ain't no Butlin's. They ain't here for their health. They here because of our health.'

'I asked where it itched,' Rupert repeats deliberately, ignoring Kwate's bark.

'You are something else,' Kwate says.

'All right, tell me,' Rupert insists to the girl.

'Down my back. Oh, please let me put my arms down.'

'I said shut up!' Kwate kicks the divan, but it doesn't make the noise he expects.

'Let her put her arms down,' Hurly says.

'We don't want no argument. I'm going to scratch

your back for yuh,' Rupert says, and getting up he walks up to the girl. He sticks the gun in her back and moves it up and down against her flesh.

'Where you say it itches?'

'Please,' she says. 'Please.' There are circles of dried sweat on her white blouse under her armpits, and the small muscles of her neck look fragile under the light down of her blonde hair.

'All right, your arms down.'

'Not you all, just she,' Kwate says, trying to remain in charge.

'Let them sit like that, they can't do us nothing,' Hurly says.

'All right, ten minutes' recess,' Kwate says, and his voice is weary. Sleeplessness is beginning to wrinkle his smooth, shiny skin. The sweat stands out in clear beads on his upper lip.

Again the voice from the loud-hailer floats up. 'You all must be hungry, Kwate. How much food have you got?'

No answer.

There is the sound of consultation once more and a voice, this time in clear cockney, asks: 'Oi, Quatty, do you agree to accept some food? We've brought up some steaming hot soup, and some snout. Let the hostages have 'em if you don't want 'em.'

'Tell them no, to blood clot. It's Bully, innit?'

'We should give them something, I feel,' Hurly says.

'Aw, come on, we eat nothing from when we come up here,' the Greek man says, turning round on his stool now, his eyes making sure that none of the gunmen will be goaded into using their hardware. 'Police say want food, we take it, yes?'

Rupert has earlier brought out all there was in the kitchen and laid it on the floor for Kwate's inspection : a packet of damp biscuits, four eggs, a couple of slices of mildewed bread and a pat of rancid butter. They are still in a corner of the room where Rupert left them.

'If we take the soup we can make them drink it first to see if it's poison,' Hurly says.

'What do you say, boys?' PC Bully shouts up again.

'Friend and benefactor of wayward boys, the man Bully,' Rupert says.

'All right, send it up,' Kwate shouts back. 'Don't forget the fags, and if you try some trick you could send one food less for the hostages. You try anything and one of them won't be needing food at all, at all.'

In the next ten minutes the tray of soup is in the room with four packs of cigarettes. The police leave the soup in the corridor. They hear the man come up to the top of the stairs and descend again. Hurly counts his footsteps. He counts twenty eight. He says to himself that he'll store the information in his head. He remembers that his father once said to him, 'Don't forget nothing. Count the inches a man made of, then you know his size.'

Rupert goes to fetch the tray when Kwate indicates with a jerk of his head that he can. Hurly, watching Kwate and keeping his revolver trained on the white man, gets to his feet and moves to the door behind Rupert, trying to give Kwate the impression that he is going to cover Rupert's return down the corridor. He sticks his head out. He wants to see if the corridor has a skylight. He wants to look around every crevice of their cage.

He watches Rupert moving cautiously, almost on

tiptoe. The corridor looks strange, as though Hurly has never seen it before. There's no skylight, but there's a little window at the top of the stairs. It looks much shorter than it did earlier, Hurly thinks, when they rushed up the stairs, pushing the hostages in front of them. Kwate had paused at the top of the stairs, holding the Greek man while Rupert and Hurly had run the girl and the younger man through into this room. Hurly had left them with Rupert and gone down the corridor again to grab the child who was struggling with Kwate, trying to get his father loose from Kwate's grip. Hurly remembers the panic, the feeling of being up against the wall, as Kwate screamed at the police who were below the turn of the stairs. He was ordering them down and his threats, in spite of his screams, were cool and clear.

'We is armed. We all got gun. I'm going to blast you to blood if you don't back up.'

Hurly heard them scrambling down the stairs, the two P.C.s who had got out of their car just as the three of them had tried to make a break out of the door with the bag of money. They must have radioed for help, Hurly thought.

It's all gone wrong, the whole bloody thing. But the police will have to give in in the end, Hurly tells himself. The desperate scramble up the stairs seems like a nightmare now, the pushing and pulling and clutching the arms of the white man who had refused to turn round and have the gun conveniently in his back. Hurly had made him walk backwards up the stairs as soon as the heat of the wrestle had turned into the cold fear of the shining black pistol, of its compact but gaping authority. The fat Greek man had held onto Kwate's neck like a man scrambling onto a life-boat in a choppy sea. They had made the hostages lie down on the floor, and the girl had started crying, long, slow, almost inaudible gasps and sobs. Hurly was still not sure that the hostages understood what had happened. It was a mistake. He could see Rupert, the exhaustion of the first moments gone, blinking his long eyelashes, looking from Kwate to the four figures lying on their bellies in the centre of the room. He could see that even Rupert wanted to say something to the hostages, but neither of them dared in front of Kwate. Kwate couldn't stop himself barking threats at the hostages.

'Hush up,' Hurly said to him, but accepted Kwate's command to stand by the door, to look into the kitchen, to take particular positions around the hostages.

Hurly hands out the soup, watching the hostages as they turn on their stools, as instructed, to eat, clutching the metal mugs with both hands to restore some of the warmth that sitting still has drained out of them. The Greek man begins to speak to his son for the first time now.

'What's your names?' Hurly asks.

'Photopoulos,' the Greek man answers. 'Is my son here, Panos.'

'Cut that nonsense,' Kwate says, rising.

'It's best we know their names,' Hurly protests.

'Rest it. This ain't social security, asking people them private business.'

Kwate's tone tells Hurly that he is determined to give orders. He is the oldest; he has masterminded the whole mess. Hurly thinks he knows how to handle Kwate. They have to keep him cool. I know Kwate as Rupert don't know him, he thinks. There's always a reason for Kwate's temper. OK, he's right. We shouldn't get friendly with these people. It's us or them, after all, Hurly thinks.

Then as though Kwate has been reading his mind, he says, 'It's not us and these here, it's us and the whole Babylon. Them out there. You got a piece of Babylon in here and you hold it the distance of a bullet, boy, don't go asking names and stupidness.'

'The Queen versus the Queen's niggers,' Rupert says.

As the night wears on, Hurly can feel the sleep crawling from the back of his skull. The words of a reggae tune keep going round in his head. '*The righteous shall stand and the weak heart drop*,' he says, staring at the ceiling and rocking on the back legs of his chair.

'If it's the Bible you're after quoting,' Rupert says, parodying his mum, 'you'd best remember your strongest prayers.'

Two

'Why ain't there no food here?' Kwate asks the Greek man.

'Nobody want work weekends. Only for plenty money. So nobody stay here. I was waiting till all the money come in on Friday night; all drivers come for money Friday. Is pay day.'

'All right leave it,' Kwate says.

The Greek man won't leave it. A direct question gives him the chance to reach out with words to his captors. All day his eyes have been trying to search their faces for some point of contact with them.

'If they want work overtime, then they tells me Friday night. If they don't, then too bad.' He shrugs his shoulders and smiles. 'No white man want to work Saturday. Only Greek, Jamaican, Paki drivers work Saturday.'

'What were you doing here?' Hurly asks the white man.

The man looks at the girl. 'She's my girl-friend.' Only for an instant does he take his eyes off the guns.

'So, did we ask you for a marriage certificate?' Rupert says. 'My spa here asked a simple question.'

'I work here. I was sitting playing cards with Photo when you came to pay us a call,' the man says, with an edge of insolence in his voice.

'So what's she doing here?' Rupert asks.

'Search me. You brought her up here.'

Hurly sees that the white man is tense and the tension makes him talk faster, speeding up his drawl. He looks into the man's blue eyes which refuse to look back. His adam's apple jumps under the unshaved stubble on his neck.

'So you were going to have a little bap-de-bap with the lady here?' Rupert says.

'I stay the night sometimes. I live down Bromley, and if it's late I hole up here. It's a kind of waiting room.'

'So you make him wait?' Rupert asks, turning to the girl.

Hurly feels that Rupert is pushing them too far. He watches Rupert and can see that there's an uncertainty about his smart talk. He's putting on this bullying to prove to himself that he's not afraid of these people. Especially the white man. He's the sort of white man who would lick you down first and then ask questions. Hurly can sense that the white man is uneasy. He, too, can see that these three pairs of eyes have singled him out as potential danger.

The girl looks nervously at the white man. She looks uncertain, as though she doesn't know whether to reply to Rupert or not.

'I wish I hadn't stayed for that game with Photo now,' the white man says.

'I wish I was Mao Tse-tung,' Rupert replies. 'No, not him, I wish I was, what's that daft millionaire's name in the States? The guy who locks himself up in one room with his friends, and his friends turned out to be enemies? Howard somethink.'

'Howard Hughes,' the white man says.

'Yeah, him. We coulda be rich today if you didn't shoot your mouth off. What you had to lose? It's your money?'

'I should be so lucky. It's the company's money.'

'So you guard it like Judas' treasure?'

'I wasn't to know what you was up to, was I?'

'Stop mess with them. No talk,' Kwate interrupts.

'No names, no talk, what is this? You figure how we going out? Them should talk a bit to us, you know, like pay their way, do a lickle drama or something,' Rupert says.

'Who drop the money?' Kwate now asks.

Rupert had been carrying the bag as they started to make their way out of the little office downstairs. They had made too much noise smashing the lock, forcing the doors of the cupboard in which Slingo said the money was kept. The money was there all right. If they had been half a minute faster, they could have got away with it. So enter the white man. He had come running down the stairs followed by the Greek man, the girl and the child who all began to shout when they realised that Rupert had gone out of the door with the money. For an instant, Kwate had attempted to bluff. He caught the man at the bottom of the stairs.

'We have to bang all night to get a cab in this place?' he had asked. And then, 'If you've closed up you shouldn't leave the light on.'

The white man hadn't hesitated for a moment. He looked past Kwate, and pushing him with his elbow in his neck, he ran after Rupert into the street. Kwate was thrown off balance and the Greek man saw the shotgun which Kwate was holding behind his back. He threw himself on Kwate and tried to wrestle him for it.

Then Rupert came rushing back into the shop, still trying to fight off the white man. The next thing Hurly knew was that Kwate had jerked free with a shout and rushed to the door, pushing Rupert and the white man.

Hurly had taken two steps to follow when the police car screeched to a halt at the kerb and the two policemen jumped out. Hurly had taken the initiative. 'Back up the stairs,' he shouted to the girl and the child, and Rupert and Kwate had dashed past him. herding the white man and the Greek at gunpoint.

Rupert can't remember dropping the money. He knows that Kwate's question is directed at him to make him shut up. He goes back to his station now, the chair between the two doors. They have boarded up the kitchen window by pushing the rickety kitchen cupboard up against it and piling the table on top of the cupboard. The kitchen leads to a miserable hole of a toilet, a little boxed-in square without a window.

The faces of the hostages are not very clear from where Rupert is sitting. His ear is on the corridor and the stairs beyond. The child has said nothing. He looks at his father who pats his hand periodically, and says to them, 'You look fine boys to me. Nothing against black myself, everybody is same. Lots of Jamaican drivers work for me. but I not the boss, eh? Is not my money. I'm a worker. Pay rent, pay tax, gas, electricity, nothing left, eh?' He turns the cloth lining of his jacket pockets out. Rupert can see that though he is trying to make them feel at ease with him. the man is terrified, not of him, but of Kwate.

Kwate has decided that a message must be sent out demanding a deal with the police. They will go to Algeria. They will ask for safe conduct to Heathrow airport and carry their hostages with them. Hurly doesn't know where Algeria is, but Kwate says that they are on the side of terrorists, revolutionaries, anyone who strikes a blow for the oppressed of the world.

'What you for and what you against?' Kwate demands.

'Isn't Algeria Communist?' Rupert asks.

'Communist wouldn't have an ambassador in Babylon. Them countries is dread, and they wouldn't send nobody here or they get the chop as spies,' Hurley says.

'Leave the politics to I,' Kwate says. 'Just write the note.'

'We have to write two notes. One to the Algerian ambassador, one to the po-lis,' Rupert says.

'We could go to Africa from there,' Hurly ventures.

'It is in Africa.' Rupert looks at Hurly as though he is a school-mate giving stupid answers in class.

'No. I mean to our own people,' Hurly explains.

'You mean Brockley,' Rupert says.

'Don't jester,' Hurly says. Kwate looks around the room for something to write with.

'We should call the Jamaican ambassador,' Hurly tries hopefully.

'He's called the High Commissioner,' Rupert says. 'We want to send it to the High Commission.'

'There would be a whole heap of pressure on those dogs from the people. Jack them up. They'd have to think before refusing us. I never buy a passport for nothing,' Kwate says.

'What people?' Rupert asks.

'The masses,' Hurly replies, thinking he's gauged Kwate's meaning.

It seems to Rupert as though nothing has been decided. They've written the note. It says: *We demand a plane at Heathrow airport with a black pilot and crew to take us to Algeria without refuelling stops. We demand to see the Algeria representative and the Jamaican*

21

High Commissioner, who is empowered to negotiate with us. We are going to shoot one of the hostages if you don't agree. This deadline expires at noon.

Now there's an argument about how to sign it. Rupert wants to leave it unsigned, and Hurly wants to sign it *The Freedom Fighters*. Kwate decides. It will be left unsigned. Kwate gets Rupert to read the note to the hostages.

'You doing a wrong thing there,' the Greek man says.

'Can we write notes out to our relatives? We can say you're treating us well. It'll be good for your propaganda, you know,' the white man offers.

'Eh-eh, I ain't allowing no code and thing to pass this window. Next we know they'll come crashing through the door.'

'The world will end with bang bang and not with whisper,' Hurly pronounces, opening his revolver, pulling the bullet out of the chamber and blowing through the barrel. He feels the weight of the bullet for the first time.

'What's that?' Rupert asks.

'That's what the poet say. They tell us that in school.'

As dawn breaks it begins to drizzle. The hostages are allowed to go to the toilet, one by one. The note is thrown out of the window. Kwate has Hurly guard the hostages as they pass through the kitchen, the child first, the girl, the white man and then the Greek man. A silent procession. They have heard the death warrant that these boys have pronounced on them, and alone in the kitchen with each of them, Hurly feels awkward. The girl tries to smile, a weak, unsure smile. Hurly doesn't want to smile back. Kwate is right. We shouldn't get friendly with these people. If they're in dead trouble, so are we, Hurly thinks. For all he knows, one of them is going to have to shoot one of these people tomorrow. And yet he wants to convince them, the girl, the Greek man, even the child, that he is not being mean, that he's doing what he has to do, he's just trying to remain private, to keep his anxieties to himself.

The white man throws a glance at him as the girl leaves. He has singled me out as the soft one of us three, Hurly thinks. Rupert plays tough but he isn't really tough. He's keeping himself going with all his smart talk, but he'll crack sooner than me. It's funny watching this white man going to the toilet, forcing him to leave the door slightly ajar as Kwate has instructed. The man don't show any fear, he hides it like all white men do, Hurly thinks, with a twinge of admiration. And yet he can smell the anxiety off him, and off the Greek man.

Years ago his mother told him that cats never die in the house. They go out and choose their resting place because they don't want to bother the people who've kept them alive, with the inconvenience and terror of death. He remembers hearing also, somewhere, maybe in school, that elephants bury themselves before they die. If they killed one of these hostages, what would they do with the body? Blood and stink and horror, Hurly thinks, people have to bear each other's blood and stink and fear. Maybe you can bear that in your family, with people you love, you can take on the idea of their death, but the smell of anxiety that comes off these people, the hostages, even off Kwate and Rupert, it's the stink of strangers. Any moment those fears might break out into panic. What could he do, or Kwate do with his cool and his calculation? They were messing with something that was beyond calculation here. They were caught up in a drama without a plot. They would each have to learn how to be completely private, to prevent trapping the others in fear, like the fear of soldiers in a trench war, your own side and the other side, all those Germans stumbling in the mud with barbed wire in their guts, bleeding, sweaty shirts and gaping mouths.

It was stupid wanting to sign the note *Freedom Fighters*. What sort of freedom were they fighting for now? We have to find a way of living with these people and not being bothered by their stink, and that's freedom, Hurly thinks.

Over the loud-hailer comes Burgess's voice: 'Boys, we've got your note.'

Three

Before they will give any reply to the demands, the police want confirmation of the names of the hostages.

'I don't want to give my name,' the girl says.

'I ain't want your name,' Kwate says. 'You are the Greek man and that's your chile, and we have here a beast-man and his piece. No names.' He has been careful to call 'oi' when he wants Rupert or Hurly. 'I the only person with a name. Just call me Kwate.'

'You hear now, don't call us all John, either,' Rupert says.

'Write it down on a piece of paper, your names and addresses,' Kwate commands.

'My dad don't know I'm here,' the girl says. The circles of half-sleep have begun to mark her eyes.

'You just write it,' Kwate says handing her a sheet of paper. 'Can you write?' he asks the white man, and then for the first time grins.

One after the other the hostages sign. The child gets hold of the paper and puts it on the floor. His father looks over his shoulder. Kwate glances at the sheet, folds it up carelessly, winds it around the handle of one of the police mugs and throws it, clattering, to the street below.

Rupert walks around the room and opens the drawers of the writing desk. 'Where you put the pack of cards?' he asks Hurly who tidied up the room the previous day.

Out of the drawer comes a pack of cards, a box over-

25

flowing with cigarette coupons, some account books and a thick text bound in yellow.

'What's this book?' Rupert asks the white man.

'It's my book,' the man replies.

'So, I ain't stealing it,' Rupert says. 'You want to call me a thief?' He leafs through the book. It's called *I Ching.*

'You interested in Kung Fu?' he asks the white man.

'Nothing to do with Kung Fu, mate,' the man replies.

'It's a Chiney book, isn't it?' Rupert thumbs through it. 'What you do with this book?'

'Read it.'

Rupert turns to look at the man. This is too cheeky, he feels.

'Is for fortunes,' the Greek man says, 'he tell fortunes with it. Your luck for the days.'

Rupert nods, accepting that as a satisfactory answer. He opens the book at random and reads:

> *The best man in his dwelling loves the earth*
> *In his heart he loves what is profound*
> *In his associations he loves humanity*
> *In his words he loves faithfulness*
> *In government he loves order*
> *In handling affairs he loves competence*
> *In his activities he loves timelessness.*
> *It is because he does not compete that*
> *   he is without reproach.*

'This is a true book,' Rupert says. He scratches the back of his head ritualistically. *Competence, timelessness, faithfulness*: he tries to absorb the ideas. Little bags under his eyes bunch up as he squints at the paper. Edwina always says that he looks like a child when he's reading, amazed that the print can trap his mind.

'What did your fortunes say?' he asks the white man.

'It said I'd be in deep trouble,' the white man answers. Rupert looks at him, stares into his startlingly light blue eyes, lets his eyes roam slowly over his tartan lumbershirt and tight jeans. The man dresses younger than he is, he thinks.

'Your stars must be the same to mine. I'm in dead trouble and all.'

'Not when you're still holding the gun, mate,' the man says. It reminds Rupert of what the white kids in the drama group used to say: 'What do you call a nigger with a gun? You calls him Bwana.'

'This thing,' he says, picking up the pistol which rests on the table next to him. 'It's a passport to Algeria, eh Hurly?'

But although he speaks of it, Rupert doesn't want to think about Algeria. If only the white man understood how desperate he is to disown that gun. He hadn't been told about the guns when they were planning the robbery. Only about the money, only about the simplicity of it all. 'Liberate' the money, Kwate had said, not steal it. A thousand pounds in his pocket, and that would be a passport to a future, a way of looking forward to the next day. You could measure days by the ways in which you could spend money through them.

Rupert had seen it as a way of getting Edwina back. Not that she'd be attracted by the money. She never thought about that sort of thing. Her kind of whites took money for granted. Ever since she'd gone, he had thought the only way to get her back was to give her the idea that he was going places, give her some vision of the future with him. He would do this one job, he thought, and then he would get out of Kwate's way, out of Hurly's way. He would do it and forget them.

27

Kwate had called the robbery 'an act of survival'. You couldn't grudge people the things they had to do for 'survival'. Everything Rupert had done, his whole life up to the time he'd met Edwina, could be looked at like that — 'hustle' and 'survival'. Kwate had the knack of truth; he found words to make experience fall into line.

Six months ago, Rupert would have been down on the Portobello Road selling second-hand macs and coats. That was his last successful hustle. A white boy, Nick, a boy he'd been at school with, had taught him the trick. Nick had dreamt it up. They would dress up politely and go to Hampstead or to Dulwich, to the doors of town houses, the houses of the rich, and spin a yarn to the ladies who answered the doorbells. They'd put on a sober face and tell them that they were collecting clothes for a jumble sale in Brixton to finance a nursery school for young blacks. They would be back the next day if 'Miss' wanted to contribute anything, any old thing, like raincoats which nobody used and so on.

Rupert collected stacks of stuff; the people they tapped were suckers for the line. Then chuck all the Burberries and Gannexes into the laundromat dry-cleaner, iron them out, and take them round to the 'Bello to flog.

That was the real work, the sweat for which money was exchanged. The regular market-stall people down the Portobello had canvasses to keep the rain out and estate cars and vans in which to stash their loot. Rupert made do with an old suitcase which he'd taken from his mother and a set of piled packing-cases to display his wares.

The blacks who floated down the 'Bello would look contemptuously at him. 'What you selling there?'

At first Rupert had been terrified of them. Then, after

Slingo had moved in on him, and he got used to Slingo's cat and mouse manner, his game of constantly threatening the people he was talking with, he became more comfortable with these swaggerers. He had begun to learn, through being with Slingo and his friends, just how much of their swagger was a manner. 'You can see what I'm selling, Jah,' he would reply.

One Saturday a 'Power boy', a man with dark glasses and a beret and an imitation military jacket sauntered up to him. 'Why you want to keep the white man dry when a hard rain's gonna fall?' he said.

Rupert felt that he'd made up the line and crossed the street with the sole intention of delivering it.

'Talk to me if you've got fourteen pounds, otherwise move on,' he said to the man.

'A tough brother,' the Power boy said, in what he fancied was an American accent, 'a rough mother. I'll be seeing you when the home fires begin to burn.'

'Yeah,' Rupert said, 'and bring your fourteen pounds.'

He did his business on the right side of the tracks. Beyond the antique stalls and the throng of Saturday tourists on the Portobello Road, beyond the concrete feet of the elevated highway that seemed planted there to make a separation between rich and poor, black and white, sprawled the ghetto. There were West Indian restaurants, reggae shops, second-hand clothing stalls, stalls selling black revolutionary literature and an endless line of junk shops. At first, Rupert would do his business and go home. After Slingo moved in on him and came down occasionally to the stall where he was selling on Satuday mornings, he would venture, under Slingo's protection, into the black cafes beyond the divide. Sometimes they would meet Kwate. Slingo would talk about the hundred schemes he had of doing really good business, but Rupert knew, Kwate knew, everyone who sat around them knew, that Slingo would stop short of effort. He regarded work as sub-human activity, he wouldn't dream of doing it.

Rupert kept his own business and his plans and hustles from Slingo and from the others who hung around the squat. He didn't trust Slingo. He slept with his money under his pillow as a precaution, even though he knew that Slingo wouldn't do anything as crude as rob him. Yet it was better to be safe than sorry.

Until he met Slingo and Kwate and Hurly, he hadn't any black friends. Brixton had been a mystery to him. He would go into the market for his mother, and he would see the black gangs hanging around the record shops. He knew their reputations, and some of them he knew from school, but he kept himself aloof. Once he saw a black girl pick a woman's handbag and the girl saw him seeing her, and she smiled. He couldn't get himself to do that, he thought, he'd have to be more inventive, he'd have to be safer.

When he lost a job his mother would moan at him and she would get her husband, who wasn't Rupert's father, to 'reason with the boy', which years ago meant a belting, but now that he was older, a shouting match and a punch in the face if he was unlucky.

Since he'd quit school, Rupert had had twenty jobs. At one time he'd been a jewel-polisher in an East End firm. He'd only taken the job, out of all the others the careers' officer had suggested to him, because it sounded as if one could take advantage of other people's carelessness in such a job, pocket a diamond or two. But the guys who ran that racket knew what they were doing. They'd give you a chance to slip something under your overalls and then they'd have you. Set up and send down, that's how the world is kept honest.

He'd lost that job because the guy on the bench next to him had tried to steal an uncut stone. The man in the office said, 'We tried to teach you a skill, here, Mr Dowling, but we believe you abused our trust in abetting Andrew in his dishonest ways.'

'I never troubled the stones, Mr Conchy.'

'No, but you left your register unmarked until Andrew could fill it in. We'll leave the police out of this because no damage has been done. But please remember, after you get your cards from Tony, that wherever you work you'll be handling other people's wealth. You have to learn to distinguish what's yours from. . . .'

After that came the job of salesman at the posh leather merchant in Bond Street. One day Nick had come in, dressed in a pin-striped suit and carrying a huge paper bag of clothes he'd bought. Rupert had stuffed an identical bag with watchstraps, handbags, belts and wallets and swapped it for the 'customer's' bag of clothing. He had stayed in that job for a few more days, then told the manager that he wanted to leave as he was going to Palestine to train as a guerilla, but that he'd very much like to work in the same capacity when he returned in two months' time.

'Have a nice holiday,' the manager said. 'But since you're not eligible for leave till you've worked for at least six months, we may find that we need somebody permanent. . . .'

It was Nick who told him that he could squat a place, that it was possible to set oneself up like the hippies did by smashing through the glass of an empty house, getting oneself inside and claiming squatters' rights.

Nick had gone with him one afternoon and helped him move into the empty, four-bedroomed, damp, stinking domain. He had moved in a mattress and lived like a ghost in one of the rooms, the rest of them echoing with emptiness.

That's when he met Slingo and Kwate and the rest. He had returned from the Portobello Road one Saturday to find them already in his house. He put his key in the door and found that it didn't work. A sort of panic seized him. He thought the police had moved in and changed the lock or something. He peered through the letter-box and voices floated out of the house. A figure came down the stairs.

'What you want?' Slingo had asked.

'I live here.'

'Who it is?' a voice shouted down the stairs.

'Some lickle half-caste boy say he live here,' Slingo shouted.

'I got the key,' Rupert said, lamely.

'So that's all your stuff, upstairs?'

'Yeah, it's my stuff.'

'Well, you better get it shifted, because you don't live in this here yard no more.'

Rupert didn't know how to react. 'I got this place first.'

'I got it second,' Slingo said.

Then Kwate had come down the stairs.

'Let the boy in,' he said to Slingo, and Slingo moved aside, withdrawing his arm that barred Rupert from the door.

'I pay rent for this place,' Rupert lied.

As soon as he saw Slingo's face in that doorway, he knew that this was what he had feared from the beginning. Someone else would move in on him. In a flash

Rupert had decided that he would fight to keep his place. He couldn't turn tail and remove his things. He had nowhere to go.

Kwate had resolved it. He asked him to come upstairs.

'Let's go into your room,' Kwate had said and Rupert led them up. There were two other people in the empty room upstairs. Slingo had brought his own stuff into the house. He had changed the lock on the door. He was talking about bringing in a cooker. 'You better ask this brother,' Kwate said to Slingo. 'We didn't know the place was already squat.'

There was no hope of getting them out, Rupert thought. He addressed his remarks to Kwate whom he could see was in charge. He explained how he had moved in and lived there for six weeks.

'Now you have to share,' Kwate said. 'If this is your room, this is your room. Slingo here has the next door.'

That's how it was settled. Rupert heard Kwate tell Slingo to give the boy a key and to treat him nice, because the boy could call the police on them if he wanted. 'Don't ever call nobody half-caste,' Kwate had said, 'one grain does make the whole sea salt.'

Kwate gave him confidence. He was the only person Rupert had ever met who seemed to understand the whole jigsaw of the world and place the pieces to make an already conceived picture. Rupert learnt that Hurly was his disciple, and that Slingo, though not impressed with Kwate's advertised wisdom, hung around him because he felt he could put Kwate to use.

'The man have theory,' Hurly would say. It never became clear to Rupert what Kwate did for a living, but it seemed to him that everybody owed him favours. He would use his authority to make one person do something for another. He was a contact man.

But he was more than that. Kwate it was who had explained to Rupert, sitting in Slingo's room, and later in the cafes of Brixton or Notting Hill, why things happened the way they did. He said that slavery hadn't been abolished, that working on the buses or cleaning up white man's dirt in the hospitals was a new kind of slavery. He had some startling opinions. He told Rupert that blacks weren't hated by 'the man'. In Kwate's world picture it was 'the man' who was the power that made the world run. 'The man' loved blacks really, he loved their hands and their cotton-picking fingers and their strong muscles, because they made money for him, and you have to love your instruments. The world was made up of love and hate, and most of all it was made up of power, and people who had power, or wanted it, must know how to manipulate the love and hate of other people. When Hurly said the police were racists, Kwate argued that they weren't. They just had some misdirected hate, because really 'the man' wanted the police to treat blacks like everyone else, he wanted Babylon to do its job, which was to keep the rich that way and the poor any way they could.

Kwate declared that he didn't talk politics. Rupert had watched him argue with a white man who walked into the Portobello cafe one day and tried to sell them a newspaper of some sort. Kwate was telling him that his newspaper was no good because it didn't know who hated what and why.

The white man listened to Kwate for a bit and then said, 'The mistake you make is you don't see the classes in society, you don't see it as a class problem. The exploitation of black people is a class problem.'

34

Kwate didn't hesitate. 'It's not a class problem,' he replied, 'it's an arse problem. Too much arseholes like you try to tell black people how and when to fight.'

They had laughed. The white man had shrugged and gone away.

One Saturday, sales had been slack. A short stout Japanese man had come up to Rupert and grinned. He looked through the coats and picked out the two with the Burberry labels.

'They're nearly new.'

'What is nearly, please?'

'It's when you get close,' Rupert said, and gave the Japanese what he took to be a definition of 'nearly' with one hand almost touching the other.

'And seeing as you are an honoured guest in our country,' he continued, trying to put on his best posh accent, 'I'll give them both to you for twenty pounds.'

'Only American dollars,' the man said, smiling apologetically. He pulled out a fat wallet and began to shrug and show Rupert a wad of foreign money.

'No Anglaisy?' Rupert asked, and smiled back.

The man shook his head.

'All right, give me dollars,' Rupert said. 'How much dollars for a pound? Wait a minute.' He went over to the next stall where an Indian man was selling Japanese transistor radios.

'You know about foreign money?'

'A little.'

'How much is twenty quid in dollars?'

'From Japanese you could get forty dollars,' the Indian whispered turning suddenly conspiratorial.

'OK. All right. I'll see you right next time, old man.'

'Forty dollars,' Rupert said to the Japanese, and the man, still smiling, adjusted his camera strap on his shoulder and counted out eight notes.

On Monday, Rupert took the five-dollar bills down to the bank in Brixton. The assistant came back with the manager.

'We're very sorry, sir, but these aren't valid currency.'

'You mean bank don't change American money?'

'I mean this isn't American money. It's counterfeit. These notes are as good as Monopoly money. We've had a lot of it recently. I'm sure the police would be interested in where you acquired them. You see it's my duty to . . .'

Rupert grabbed the notes and walked out. Play money! Hustle and be hustled. He didn't expect it of the Japanese. He wouldn't have trusted a white man with this foreign money racket. How stupid, how bloody stupid. You look clean, you act dirty. How to pass these notes off on someone else? He wasn't going to the police. They'd have him for printing the money. No, he wasn't going to no police. . . .

Rupert went up to Slingo's room, the dud notes ashamedly deep in his pocket. He wouldn't tell Slingo about the Japanese man. He knew that Slingo was of the opinion that God made suckers to preserve a holy balance in the world. Slingo had theories about the smartness of different races, and the Chinese and Japanese ranked low on his scale. Once Slingo had said to him that yellow people had to invent unarmed combat like Kung Fu and Karate because they didn't have the science to put machine guns together. 'What's one better than black belt?' was Slingo's question to the young blacks who were in love with Bruce Lee and kicked and posed in imaginary victories over fabulous foes. 'Gun belt.'

'Wha' go on?' Slingo asked, reclining on his bed, the record player booming out its endless combination of *Natty* and *dread* and *Babylon* and *Jah-Jah* and *Rasta don't do this or Rasta do that.*

'Nothing much, I there,' Rupert replied, with studied laziness. With Slingo he talked as Slingo would. At first Rupert had felt a bit awkward adopting Slingo's phrases and his slurring speech, but surrounded by lads who belted it out and competed with each other for the possession of the latest phrase, he had accepted it. It helped him dramatise himself when he wanted to. In arguments with Edwina he'd begin to 'talk black'. She liked him to do it. 'Tcha, I cyan't deal with that, don't mess with my head,' he'd say. He didn't feel false talking like that any more. He'd talk like that at home when he wanted to be difficult and his mother would tolerate it as she had tolerated long years of her husband's moods.

And yet Rupert knew that even Slingo, even the most far-out hustlers who hung around their squat, could talk straight English when they wanted to. Only Slingo never did. To him the very obscurity of his language, the trickiness of his accent, were sources of power. Rupert knew that Slingo enjoyed forcing him to listen carefully and concentrate on catching the drift of what he was saying. Language was identity, Rupert had learnt, even for him, a half-caste with an Irish mother and Nigerian father. Identity was power.

Four

The drama workshop had been a real 'period of development' for Rupert. More words he'd picked up, this time from Michael who ran the group. They were all right words, they made sense of the tumble of his existence. One of the youths he hung around with at the jeweller's shop had taken him to the workshop. Rupert had never taken part in anything the school had asked him to do. After the third year, when he began wearing rasta caps and going around predominantly with the blacks who lounged around the school corridors, carrying pre-release records for prestige rather than to play, treating school as a meeting place, teaching each other the rude-boy idiom of the ghetto and doing as little work as possible, he had given up running in the athletics team or bouncing a ball for the basketball teacher.

The only thing he'd ever done for the school play was sit at the back of the audience and laugh uproariously at the wrong moments till the lights were switched on and he and his mob were marched off to the head's office, protesting that blacks weren't even allowed to enjoy Shakespeare in that school. But his friend told him that there were lots of black girls in the drama group, and that induced him to give it a try.

His notions of it changed with the first visit. He found he liked Michael, and Edwina, his wife, who ran the group with him. Edwina was a teacher at a school near the workshop, which was held in a youth centre called the Rampant Project. She was the mastermind of Tuesday evenings, even though it was Michael who got them all round in a circle to begin each session and help them to discuss different things with as much freedom and complication as they could muster. It wasn't like school. The seriousness of the old members of the group was contagious. They would act out the little skits and improvisations on a theme which followed, with all the vanity of footballers entering the arena, eye on object, ear on approval.

After a few Tuesdays Rupert felt easy with the group, even though there was a lingering feeling that those who asked you to put your anxieties or hang-ups into words were in some way trying to control you. Yet Edwina and Michael were pretty straightforward themselves, or at least Michael was. Behind his gold-rimmed glasses, his sincere eyes seemed always wide open in utter frankness. And when they all talked in the pub afterwards, Rupert discovered that the talk continued, that most of the group saw each other and knew each other outside the circle of chairs and props that formed their Tuesday evenings.

The group had sat back with a sort of embarrassed expectancy the day Michael began a session by stating flatly that he and Edwina had 'decided to split'. They had talked it over – what else could they do? – and they had decided that it was their duty to tell the drama group. All right, he had to admit that they had treated some of the group's confessions as kids' stuff, he was willing to say that now, but they both felt that they had grown up together over a year or more – yes, I've got grey hairs but you never stop growing – but they would like to tell the group exactly, or as best they could, what conclusions they had come to.

A hush fell over the fourteen people assembled there. Usually when one of them was struggling to say something difficult, the rest of them encouraged him or her, bantering and making jokes to steer the atmosphere away from that of a psychiatrist's couch or of a priest's confessional. Michael gulped several times during his monologue.

One of the girls asked if that meant an end to the drama group.

'No, we've decided to carry on with the group. I hope you want us to, I mean all of you. I don't want anyone to misunderstand. We aren't parading private miseries in front of you. We've known each other – how long, Edwina? – five years, and we're not getting a divorce or anything hasty like that; we just feel we haven't put our energies into exploring other people. It's a wide world, and we live in London and the city may be a dark satanic mill, but it's also a possibility of souls. Something has made us stale, I wish I knew what. So we've decided to try and live our own. . . .'

The group was waiting for Edwina's interruption. Some of them knew that Michael had a neat way of imposing explanations on people. Edwina was warmer.

'Michael's right, there's no need to split from the group, even though we're both sure you can carry it on on your own.'

There was a chorus of 'Naw'.

'Thank you, fans,' Edwina said, waving her arms. 'We've always insisted that you dig into yourselves like mines, and it's our turn to put the cards on the table, see?'

They saw. Michael said, 'So shall we work out today why exactly people get stale for each other?'

One of the girls began to giggle.

'OK, so we're funny,' Michael said. 'And if we are, you're entitled to laugh.'

'It's not that,' the girl said. 'It's my mum and dad. Mum's always saying to him, "You smell bad, bad, man, and you don't leave no cash for the children, as though I don't have to put up with your rubber smell all me life." Dad works in the rubber place up Harlesden.'

'That's a pretty straightforward reason for splitting. I ought to say Ed stinks of kids, at least her mentality does.'

They took it as a feeble joke.

'Marriage is a convenience,' Rupert contributed, looking at Edwina. It was what she had said to him the last time she was at his place.

'A public convenience,' Michael said, and there was a pause before someone suggested that they should talk in groups about how you get bored with people you've known for a long time.

Both Michael and Edwina avoided being in the same group as Rupert that session. When they were going to the pub, Edwina said quickly to Rupert that she'd see him later, at his place. She had never openly been there. She told him that Michael didn't ask her where she went.

Rupert had never wanted to deceive Michael. At first, soon after he begun to go to the drama group, he and Edwina became friends, but there was always something in their relationship which made Michael react with contempt. Rupert would go to their place and listen to records, and smoke with Edwina while Michael sat in his room and pretended to work, figuring out school syllabuses and writing for the journals to which he contributed. Then Rupert began to meet Edwina after her work. They would mostly talk about the people in the drama group, but often they would talk black politics. Edwina assumed instantly that Rupert would have something to say about them. For her he began to make up complications about his life which didn't exist. He would talk to her about the tragedy of being a half-caste, and she would listen. He learnt through her and Michael that even sincerity was a weapon, a hustle. He was flattered by her attention and turned his mind to anything that would get it.

She, in turn, would talk about herself, about how her mother who never even told her who her real father was, was ashamed of having a bastard child. She told him that she was called Edwina because her mother had 'middle-class hang-ups'. She said ever since she'd read some book or the other she wanted to be called 'George', but then decided that 'Ed' would do, and now women's liberation had taught her to be proud of her own name.

He had never met anyone like her. Once or twice, when he sat up late at their flat, she drove him home. Rupert had kept her a secret from the daily round of people he met, but in his thoughts he lived for her. He was nineteen. She was five years older. He knew she had fancy friends who had nothing to do with the drama group, with the kids she met at school. Rupert sensed also that she was fascinated by the fact that he lived in the squat. She'd asked him how he'd broken in. She questioned him about Slingo, and when Rupert threw bits of Slingo's phrases into the conversation she would ask him to explain the words. He took her reggae LPs from Slingo's battered and scratched and ever-renewed collection, and he told her stories that he'd picked up from Slingo and his mates and put himself into them.

Edwina had made the first move. She had dropped him home after the group session one Tuesday. She'd seemed preoccupied. He went to bed and two hours later heard the thud of pebbles against his window. She was back.

'Can I come in, Rupert?' she asked, looking up from the pavement, standing next to her car. She'd left the engine running.

'What's the problem?' he said, putting on his jeans and shirt before going down.

'Plenty.'

'I thought you said nothing bothered you.'

'Well, I'll have to think again, won't I?'

She came up to his room and settled herself on the mattress. She took in its complete disorder, the absence of furniture, the clothes piled in corners and the bed with threadbare blankets.

She asked for some coffee and he made her some, muttering an excuse for having only condensed milk.

'I've had a terrible argument with Michael. He's got a girl in the flat.'

'I thought that sort of thing didn't bother you.'

'Yeah, that's easy to say, isn't it. That sort of thing spoils my sleep. I don't want to go back to separate bedrooms and him sneaking off to Croydon in the morning. I can't stand the look in his eyes in the morning. It almost hurts him more than it hurts me.'

I like to be hurt like that,' Rupert said.

'Can I stay here, though? I won't if you can't handle it.'

Her face was partly covered by the strands of her thick wavy brown hair. Rupert didn't know if she was telling the truth, but he knew she had come to him.

'Do you have an alarm clock?'

'No.'

'Oh well, we'll have to stay awake all night and talk,

so I can be on time for work.' She said that and smiled. There was a kind of mock sadness in her smile. He watched her as she took her clothes off and threw them in a pile, and, striding nimbly, climbed under his blankets. It was as though she had done this little act in a hundred unfamiliar rooms before, Rupert thought.

'Sorry to have woken you up with my troubles. Stop frowning and come to sleep. Too late to throw me out now.'

He was about to say that he didn't want to throw her out, that it would be like refusing a winning ticket on the pools, but his words stuck in his throat. She was thinner than he had imagined her and her breasts hung lower than he had thought they would. His heart thumped furiously.

'Shall I switch the light off?' he asked huskily, and then, trying to cover his embarrassment, 'So that you can sleep if you're tired.'

She laughed, her arms behind her head on the unclothed pillow. 'No. Let's have a look at you.'

When he thought of that first time she had slept with him, Rupert could remember the furious thumping of his heart, the shiveriness that came over him, and the hunger of his eyes, wanting to take her in and imprint the images of her on his brain. Yet he didn't want her to do the same. He was ashamed of his bony, hairy legs that stilted out under his shirt, his sweaty hands, his pounding chest. They were confessions of inexperience.

Edwina was so different from the black girls he had known. She declared who she was and what she wanted, like a man, whereas the girls he had known had to be worked on and worked at. There was no coyness about Edwina. Rupert decided she had the kind of maturity he liked.

It was the first time that he had a woman in the squat. He had known girls in school. One or two of the girls at the drama group fancied him, or so the rest of them said, but they were the sort of girls who would challenge him to ask them out and then refuse to go, or make fun of him and his choice of film or Wimpy bar afterwards. Edwina had ideas about the world. These other girls only had a bitchiness about the people immediately around them.

It had been beautiful in the beginning. Edwina would come to his place once or twice a week. He would stay in and wait for her. He had wondered whether any of the others in the drama group suspected, when Michael came out with all that confession about breaking up, that he was involved in it.

Up until that day, Edwina would spend the night with him and would disappear in the mornings, carrying a change of clothes with her in a canvas bag like a waif. Sometimes she'd come in the evenings and take him for a drive. They'd go to the pubs by the river out in the west of London, a London he didn't know existed. She knew all sorts of places to eat and to drink and to go and watch plays in.

Rupert had a sense of inadequacy with her. She would tease him : treat him like her baby, like her eldest son with whom she had a 'talking relationship' as she called it, when she was with him alone, and like her tiger on a leash when they were in public. She would talk about the books she'd read and about the architecture of the houses she stopped to stare at. He hated to bring her back to the dirty squat at night.

Although he hardly admitted it to himself, he felt possessive about her. She seemed hungry for the world of noises and arguments beyond the wall of his room, but if Slingo's friends, who went with black girls and brought them up to the house to make noisy love in Slingo's room, found out about Edwina, Rupert felt his position with them would become shaky. He kept her hidden like a weakness, and day-dreamed about being able to take her away from it all one day. He would buy a house, like the one beside the river, and keep her amidst his sound system and his Lamborghini, like white people kept white, long-haired Persian cats.

When she found out that Rupert was out of a job, Edwina talked him into going to sign on at the Social Security. He didn't know anything about it and she had patiently explained it all. He went one morning and sat for three hours in the queue and answered the questions the girl put to him.

When he got back home, Slingo shouted out to him, 'Where you been?'

Rupert didn't want to tell Slingo that he'd been down to draw dole. That would be an admission of defeat.

'Why your girl-friend never speak to me?' Slingo asked.

'You ask her.' Rupert shrugged.

'She nice, you know. She's a fit daughter.' Slingo always referred to women as 'daughters'. 'Does she wan' make some breads?'

'Not with you, Slingo, I doubt it,' Rupert said, trying to turn and walk off. 'If you're giving it away, I'm starting a pension fund for old-age bag snatchers.'

'Come here, nuh, jus' make me sight you.'

Rupert went back. Something in Slingo's tone told him that Slingo was engaged in thinking, a rare occurrence, and he wanted to witness it.

'Listen. You know Kwate, yeah? He's a photographer,

and he and you and the chick could work some scene.'

'No, no scenes for her, boy, just keep her out of any-thing you plan, all right?'

'Just hear the plan one time. Is a lot of donzai in it.'

'How much?'

'Hold on there. Kwate, he's cool, you know, a political Joe, and we need a white chick who understands things, like.'

'What things? She hasn't got any credit cards or cheque books or nothing, I tell you.'

'One day's work. Black man, white woman, tiger skin, have a little scene, mix business with pleasure, sell the film and split the donz.'

'I don't think she'd do it.'

Slingo propped himself up on his elbow and showed his black tooth in an evil smile. 'You mean you couldn't control she?' There was a sort of sympathy in Slingo's voice, but Rupert knew it was blackmail, gently applied. 'She give you a lot of horrors, I hear.'

'Naw, she's a decent girl, straight. She wouldn't fancy making no sex films.'

'You don't ask she what she fancy, man, you tell her. It's your woman, isn't it? Give her little soft talks. You is a man always popping it on white woman.'

'Maybe, but I don't treat her like that. She used to be my teacher, man. That's using people.'

Slingo sucked the air through his teeth, making his spit screech in derision. He sank back on the bed.

'I will ask she,' he announced to the room.

Slingo's proposition worried Rupert. It added a dis-turbing sediment to his already cloudy mind. It made him wish he didn't live there any longer. Undoubtedly Slingo would carry out his threat and ask Edwina if she'd perform in his proposed film. He was sure it was Slingo's idea. Kwate, he thought, wouldn't get involved in that sort of scene.

Edwina didn't turn up that evening. Just before midnight Rupert heard Slingo leave the house, a cat on the night prowl. Perhaps by the next day he would have forgotten his plan. He would only remember it when he wanted to taunt Rupert with being a white man, with having an incoherent morality beneath the skin.

They were all like that, Slingo's mob. Except, perhaps, Kwate, who was more thoughtful. Kwate was the only one out of the dozens of boys who visited the house, lounged and slept and ate there, with whom Rupert felt he could talk. Kwate didn't throw words around; he was much more deliberate. And yet he knew that Kwate, too, was capable of wild action. Not of small-time hustles. Kwate was distinctly big-time.

Five

There is no reply from the police through the second night of the siege, and hostages and gunmen sit through the next morning, waiting.

'My watch stop,' Hurly declares. 'When I don't sleep I forget to wind it.'

'What's the time? Give me the time,' Kwate says to the hostages who are sitting on the settee now, bleary-eyed but alert. Kwate faces them with the shotgun.

'Eleven,' the white man says. He looks more bored than terrified now, as though he feels that his captors and the police are handling the whole thing in too tedious a fashion and he could have planned the moves of either side much better.

'So they don't care for the deadline,' Rupert says.

'The embassies will have just opened, they'll need time,' the girl says. 'Oh God, I wish I'd never . . .'

'The old bill are up to no good as usual. Give them time,' the white man interjects. 'They couldn't organise a piss-up in a brewery.'

'We'll do our own countdown,' Kwate snaps. 'The po-lis working on your time.'

The white man shrugs and looks away from Kwate towards the window.

The deadline of noon approaches. None of them has had more than a few minutes of sleep at a time, and yet they are all as alert as jockeys in a race. Rupert and Hurly hold their pistols indifferently, as though these are no longer part of the dialogue between them and the hostages. I'm not doing any shooting, Hurly thinks. He knows that despite Kwate's unflinching stare and hardened, determined features, he isn't either.

The next time Kwate demands the time, it's ten to one.

The Greek man licks his lips and asks for water. Kwate says he can go to the kitchen and get some, and he motions to Rupert to stay where he is, even though Rupert springs up to follow the Greek.

The girl begins to say something to the white man. She whispers, but they can all hear what she says.

'How long it take to send a telegram to Algeria?' Kwate asks, forestalling her.

'It might take a whole day,' the white man replies.

Kwate lifts the shotgun in both hands when he throws his arms up theatrically in a yawn. Rupert watches him and thinks he looks like the guerrilla in the poster and wants to look like him.

At four o'clock the police break their silence.

'Kwate, we've received your demands and want to install a phone so you can talk to us direct. There are some difficulties about your demands.'

They think we're not serious, Hurly thinks. We didn't shoot anybody, we couldn't shoot anybody. Maybe they'll come for us. It's like waiting on death row. He recalls all those telly films about guys going to the electric chair or the gas chamber or the gallows, with the good guys outside, the lawyers and reporters who valiantly spend sleepless nights looking for last minute evidence, and the careful preparations inside, the death hoods, the glass jar of the gas chamber, the straps on the chair, and the echoes of steel doors, the echoes of bunches of keys and the echoes of the boots of dutiful screws.

When they watched these programmes in Slingo's room, Kwate would say, 'The wolf will lie down with the lamb – in he belly.' He'd say that about almost any programme, but now suddenly it seemed to make sense. Those death row movies, with their horrid fascination, were a preparation for all the waiting games one had to play. Time has come, Hurly thinks, only there'll be no reprieves and no last minute pardons; it's a game of chess in which black starts second and always loses.

'Go talk to them,' Kwate says to Rupert.

Rupert looks out of the window as Kwate shouts, 'We coming to the window. If you try something, someone going to dead.'

Rupert sees police cars and vans at either end of the street. The camera crews are standing around with electronic headgear, smoking and drinking from paper cups. The spectators throng behind a scanty line of uniformed bobbies. There are black faces in the crowd. The curtains of most of the flats in the white stuccoed terrace opposite, are drawn. On the morning of the first day of the siege, the police took charge of these rooms and ordered the inhabitants out of them, but there's no way Rupert can know that. As soon as his face appears at the window there's a cry from the crowd, and Rupert ducks back in.

'Tell them we want newspapers,' Kwate says. Rupert shouts out the message.

'Will you accept the phone?' is the police reply.

'How you go set it up?' Kwate shouts back.

Burgess doesn't understand the question. Rupert can't see Burgess who's standing almost immediately below at the door of the mini-cab shopfront, and shouting up. Rupert repeats the question several times and hears Burgess asking for help from the other police.

'All right,' Kwate shouts in the end, replacing Rupert at the window.

Burgess's voice again : 'P.C. Bully is going to bring you the telephone set on a ladder outside this window.'

'We trust him without his coat,' Kwate shouts back.

The next day in the papers one headline says GUNMEN TRUST PC BUT NOT HIS COAT. Another says UNIFORM TERRIFIES SIEGE GUNMEN.

Bully comes into view at the top of the ladder looking extremely self-conscious.

Everyone in the black community knows P.C. Bully. He is notorious for being crooked and fearless. He leans out of his squad car to shout at blacks he's arrested, 'Glad to see you walking straight, Sunshine.'

Bully goes down into the clubs and dives alone. He swears in a pseudo-Jamaican accent and puts on an ironic act of being one of the boys. The youths know him as one policeman who can come up behind them and say, 'Shift your raas clot.' Kwate has heard that the other coppers don't like Bully; they say he is angling for promotion, and they disapprove of his idea that jovial brutality is the way to handle blacks. Or perhaps they know, as blacks know, that Bully is said to be involved in big-time drug peddling, that he uses his knowledge of small-time weed dealers to track the big-timers and make deals with them. There are hundreds of rumours about Bully : that he blew up a German bunker in the war, that he was demoted in the force for bigamy, that he has been a sailor and married a woman in Anguilla. His seniors know him as a man who can spot blacks who've been in trouble previously. Burgess has asked that Bully be assigned to the siege.

Kwate puts one arm out to him. Rupert and Hurly stand beyond the kitchen doorway because Kwate says he can see through the trick of getting Bully to identify the two unknown members of their gang. Next to him, beyond the window frame, Kwate holds the white girl at gunpoint.

The phone is handed over without a word, the wire running out over the window-sill. For once, Kwate thinks, Bully isn't cocky. His bosses are watching him.

As Bully descends the ladder, Hurly and Rupert come back into the room. Kwate picks up the phone. There is an immediate reply; it's already connected. 'We want an answer to our demands and also newspapers,' Kwate says.

The crackling reply says they'll get both. Kwate puts down the phone.

'What happens if they don't give us a plane?' says Hurly.

'One by one,' Kwate says.

'We got to show we serious. Look at the paddy-men: them, they don't mess about. If IRA say they'll shoot somebody, then they spend some bullets and fetch a body.'

'The Irish have the support of their whole country,' Rupert says, echoing something he's heard Michael say.

'If a hundred po-lis rush this place, they could kill we all,' Hurly observes.

'The po-lis want them alive and us alive.'

'They can't have us for murder. Not yet,' Rupert says.

'If you get out of here, the police, the international police and all going to chase your arse right round this ungodly world,' Hurly replies.

'If we shoot somebody, they'll think we're shooting the lot and rush the place, firing.'

Late in the evening the phone rings. Hurly picks it up. It's Burgess with the answer to their demands.

'We haven't been able to get a reply from any Algerian representative. The Jamaican government will not give you asylum. There's nowhere for you to go. We urge you to give yourselves up and free the hostages.'

He goes on to say that public opinion is building up against them. He will send them the national newspapers, and, as well, newspapers from certain black groups who have all denounced them as thieves and criminals not worthy of support. If they give up the hostages now, he will personally see to it 'that all the facts are taken into account in any proceedings that might be taken against them'.

Burgess's voice can be heard in the room, straight from the ear-piece. He pauses for a reply but doesn't directly ask for one.

Wrinkles appear on Kwate's brow. He grabs the phone from Hurly's hand and bangs the receiver with his fist. 'They bug this blood-cleet thing,' he shouts.

'How can you tell?'

'I don't know how them work, but I tell you it's bugged.'

'Let's have a look,' the white man says. Kwate hands the set over to him. The man unscrews the ear-piece. He asks for a pen-knife and Kwate gets one from the pocket of his jacket. The man digs under the diaphragm, then unscrews the receiver set. All the others watch.

'It's got an extra wire, it by-passes the switch. Yeah, it's bugged all right.'

'Stand back,' Kwate says theatrically. He grabs the set from the man's hand and with tremendous venom projects it through the glass of the window.

54

There's a terrific crash as the glass and the set fall to the pavement. The sound of running feet. Captors and captives sink to the floor without a signal. They all instinctively expect something to come through the window in return. In fifteen seconds it does: the voice of Bully.

'What's going on in there, Kwate? You all OK?' He sounds almost anxious.

Kwate motions to Rupert to cover the hostages with his pistol. They are all still crouching on the floor. Kwate and Hurly up-end the table, knocking the unwashed cups, the statuette of a smiling buddha and the pack of cards onto the floor. They push the table up against the broken window, covering half of it.

Kwate stands up. 'Now they know who's serious and who's not.'

'You can't blame me,' Hurly protests. 'I don't want to kill nobody. You said it was cool to have the phone.'

'Shut up,' Kwate commands. He is now in charge completely.

'Kwate,' the white man says. They all look at him. It's the first time one of the hostages has addressed Kwate by name. The white man puts his finger on his lips for silence. He points to the window-sill, and touches his hand to his ear.

Kwate nods. The white man goes over to the window and opens it slightly. Crouching below the window frame, he runs his hand along the ledge outside.

He is right. His hand comes away with a little disc as big as a watch. He hands it to Kwate, who looks at it curiously and then, putting it on the floor, smashes it with the butt of the shotgun.

Kwate smiles at the white man.

'Who wants coffee?' Hurly asks.

55

'Let me and the girl go,' the white man says.

'You just wait where you are,' is Kwate's contemptuous reply.

The Greek man passes the photographs he's pulled out of his wallet to the other hostages.

'He looks so much younger,' the girl says, taking the measure of the boy who looks sick and miserable.

'Because he was, dumbo,' her man says.

Rupert takes the photograph from the white man's hand. The Greek comes and, leaning over his shoulder, points out who is who. In the snap the young boy is wearing a tie and a jacket and has had his hair slicked down for the occasion.

'She will be worried. Worried for nothing,' the Greek man says, indicating his fat matron of a wife. 'She will get so thin,' and he holds out his forefinger and shakes it. 'That's my big son, Costas, Panos' brother. Play very good football, school team, Cypriot team, all team. Costas nineteen now; Panos twelve.'

'Hang on, I know this geezer,' Hurly says. 'Oi, was your son a footballer?'

'Don't be so Irish, he just said he was,' Rupert says.

'Hold on there, hold on. Archway school?'

The Greek nods and his features open up, his face beaming. 'You know my son?'

'Not 'arf,' Hurly says, turning to Rupert, and adopting now his cockney voice. 'That bloke nearly kicked my ammunition off when we was playing them for the North London cup.'

'He got a big car now,' the Greek man says proudly. 'Work for this business. Mini-cabs.'

'Lucky it's not him we got here: a real nasty bruiser.

56

'Costas very good boy,' the Greek man insists, not quite catching Hurly's drift.

'Yeah. Good as a nutcracker.'

'Most night Costas he stay with me till drivers paid off. This night he go boxing, so Panos bring my supper and you boys catch us.'

'Could do with some supper now,' Rupert says.

'Call room service,' the white man says.

By the fourth day they have given up discussing killing anyone. Kwate is conscious that Rupert and Hurly are waiting for him to suggest a further plan but neither of them asks him for it. He has to be given his time.

Talking to these people Rupert has to make an effort to feel again that their lives are the only cards they hold now. He dislikes the white man. Much too flash. He wonders how a nice girl like that could go with a lout like him. He is sure that if the man had the gun and he was at the end of it, the man wouldn't hesitate to shoot.

Hurly tells the Greek man what their plan of robbery was. They have a friend, he won't say his name, who set the job up for them; it wasn't really their idea. They were told that all they had to do was go in and get the cash. It wasn't even in a safe. At the most they would find one man there and they could deal with him.

Kwate shuts Hurly up. He has established in the minds of the hostages that he is the boss, that he'll do the thinking for all three. The other two, and the hostages, behave now as though they are waiting for something to happen, but Kwate gives off the air that events are taking the turn of some carefully mapped-out route which he holds in his head.

'If it had been white people involved, the po-lis

would have given them a plane and let them loose in Australia or someplace,' he asserts.

If Hurly had said it, the white man might have said 'Don't talk daft,' but with Kwate he lets these remarks pass. Kwate rarely speaks to the hostages except through the others.

I have to trust Kwate, Rupert thinks, because there's no one else to trust. It's grudging, but it's still a convinced acceptance of Kwate's authority.

Six

Rupert had noticed that Slingo had been watching Edwina. He had mentioned the film again, to Rupert, but Rupert had fended him off.

Maybe it was just the way Slingo insinuated himself into Edwina's attention. Rupert was sure Slingo didn't know any white women apart from the girls who hung around the blues and passed from man to man, turning from unarmed amateurs into hardened professionals who knew that there was no such thing as the best bet. Slingo was fascinated by Edwina. To him she represented the conscious surrender of those who had enslaved his ancestors, or at least Rupert felt that that was how Slingo saw her. It annoyed Rupert. He was conscious that Slingo knew very well that there were at least two types of white women, and yet he persisted in treating the eagle as of the same feather as the crow.

Slingo didn't knock. He just walked into Rupert's room, hearing Edwina's voice there.

'You ask the daughter yet?'

'Ask me what?'

'You the actress, ain't yuh?'

'Well, I wouldn't exactly say . . . I'm a drama teacher.'

Her response hurt Rupert. She seemed glad of Slingo's interruption of their intimacies.

'This boy tell me a lot about you. I'm very pleased to meet you.'

'You're Slingo, aren't you. I've passed you ten times,

59

but you don't seem to look at the ghosts who pass you in this house.'

'Yeah, my mind have a lot of worries,' Slingo said. 'It's a shame this boy never tell you about some little job you could do for I.'

'Oh? What's that, Rupert? You didn't . . .'

'Slingo, leave it, man.'

'I'm making a film. I asked him if you'll play in this lickle film. It's educational.'

'How interesting. I've always wanted to make a film. In fact, you know the drama group that Rupert comes to, we're thinking of doing a film out of the sort of work we've done. We just haven't had the money. It costs an awful lot, doesn't it?'

'My spa, my friend is a producer, you know, and it have a film and breads and all. We wanted an actress so I tell Rupy to check you because he always tell me how good you was with drama.'

'Is it a black film?'

'It's black and white,' Slingo said, grinning, aware that he was making Rupert uncomfortable, aware also that Rupert would never challenge his right to say anything to any white woman in that house. 'I'm very bad at explanations. Rupert is better at explanations. Or the guy who's making this here film, Mr Brown.'

'I'd like to talk about it some time. It sounds a smashing idea.'

'You want to talk to Kwate?' Slingo said.

'Yes, I'd like that. Is he coming here some time?' Edwina sensed Rupert's shiftiness. 'Don't you think it's a great idea, Rupert? Especially if they've got film and camera and everything.'

'You may not like the script.'

'Well, I'll meet this chap, won't I. D'you know him?'

'I'm going to check him out tonight at a blues,' Slingo said, still grinning.

Rupert saw what Slingo was about. Edwina reacted to his sly invitation by sitting up on the bed.

'Kenny playing some boss sounds tonight. You want to go, Rupert?'

'I'm tired,' Rupert said, sinking back on the mattress, as Edwina sat up.

'Come on,' she cried, 'don't be such a drag. It's lovely of Slingo — I do hope that's your real name; you don't mind being called Slingo do you — to tell us about it.'

She was showing real enthusiasm. Several times she had asked him to take her where the black youths hung out. A 'reggae party' she called it. She was constantly pushing for just those things he wanted to shield her from. He could see that Slingo had sensed that and was playing on it.

'Cool, cool sound,' Slingo said.

Rupert didn't like the blues. They were carnivals of bewilderment for him. The black girls who went there were unapproachable. He felt he'd make a fool of himself if he asked a sister to dance and she ignored him and turned away. He couldn't comfort himself there — as he had done when he'd gone to the Mecca dancing halls with his white friends — with the thought that these potential partners were demonstrating their innate racism, that they wouldn't dance with him because he was black.

'If the boy tired, you'll have to come with me,' Slingo said.

'I'd really like to meet this guy,' Edwina said, turning to Rupert.

'If you want to see blues, I'll take you to blues,' Rupert said.

They went by cab. Slingo always travelled in style when there were other people who could pay. As they walked in, Edwina felt the eyes of the scattered crowd outside the church hall, upon them. Slingo seemed to know a lot of people. He had put on a red velvet jacket and wore rings on every finger. He greeted the people to-ing and fro-ing from the hall with 'All right' or 'Sights'. As they reached the door, he turned to Rupert and said, 'You have money?'

Edwina paid the white man who stood at the door in an assembly of intimidating faces. He was a vicar. He smiled at them. The sound of the party floated out into the sharp night air. Beyond the reception party, in the foyer, were a lot of young blacks with caps and totally sullen expressions, leaning against the wall and moving rhythmically to the beat at the same time. It was incredible and menacing to Edwina, and exciting at the same time. She took Rupert's arm and felt him pull away from her, a slow determined move which told her that he would keep close to her but didn't want her to claim him before that audience.

Red bulbs hung naked in the room they entered. The music seemed to quake the creaky floorboards. The place was absolutely packed out. The young men wore fancy suits, sported silk handkerchiefs, danced in a slow pounding rhythm with their coats on. A row of watchers, gazing into some deep distance, lined the walls, shuffling their feet to the music, their fists raised in gestures of loose, confident combat. The air was thick with smoke and a vaguely nauseating sweet smell.

> *Kill Pope Paul*
> *And hold the seventh seal thereof*

Kill Pope Paul
And -a- Babylon fall.

the loudspeakers blared. Rupert stood in front of
Edwina, not acknowledging her, yet sensing her depend-
ent presence just behind him. She looked round, uncertain, but keeping her chin high. The voice on the
record was almost speaking, not singing, and yet the
swaying shoulders made it sound like the most danceable
melody in the world. There was an agony and threat
in the sound which drowned everything.

Slingo wound his way through the dancers and Rupert
followed him closely. Edwina noticed that the crowd
appeared to part for them, but blocked her way as she
followed, and she was wary of saying 'excuse me' for
fear of being laughed at. Nobody excused anybody in
this crowd.

She would brave it, she thought, go in breast first,
when a voice behind her said, 'But wait.'

Edwina turned to see a young man standing behind
her, the mouth that had spoken the words almost at her
ear. He was shuffling about, moving to the rhythm with
his hands drawn up to his chest in loose fists. He met her
eye as she turned, as if to identify himself as the man
who had ventured to give her orders.

'I'm with my friends.' Edwina gestured.

'You can't go in there so,' the boy said and carried
on moving his body. 'You have no friends,' he added,
smiling.

Edwina stood transfixed. There was no going forward
through the thicket of dancers, and this boy had blocked
off her retreat. Then she noticed that no one around
them was paying the least bit of attention to what the
boy had said or to her response. The boy looked as

though he was going to push his body up against her, but he just finished his dance before he attended to the business he'd begun.

Edwina turned and tried to force herself through the dancers who closed into a wall before her.

'I said, *rest*,' the voice commanded again.

Edwina pretended she didn't hear him. To the others it must seem that she was dancing with him. She tried to concentrate on the lyrics of the song :

> *Run Cap-it-al-ist*
> *I and I want So-shyal-ist.*

Suddenly it was menacing. The man was upon her, she could smell his sweat.

> *They take an oath upon them own-a mother*
> *Then them use a gun to kill them own-a son*
> *That's why them crime canna done.*
> *It dread in a Jamdown, dread in a Jamdown. . . .*

People were pushing past her now. The song was coming to an end. As they squeezed past she saw Slingo's head above the rest. Rupert and Slingo had made their way back and with them was Kwate.

'What's happening?' Slingo said.

From behind her, the voice of the young man, no longer throaty and secret but public and matey said, 'I there.'

Kwate was introduced to Edwina and he in turn introduced them all to the boy behind her. 'Is my friend Hurlington. Wha' go on, Hurly?'

Hurly nodded. They stood around in a little circle,

and a man who passed handed Kwate a lit joint without comment. Kwate puffed at it and passed it to Hurly.

'This killer weed,' Hurly commented, looking at the thing he'd puffed, but Edwina saw a shadow of uncertainty pass across his face and she was ashamed of herself for having allowed this boy to intimidate her.

'I taken some tablet this evening,' Hurly said.

'You charged like a battery,' Slingo said, smiling, his black tooth showing through like a breach in a defence.

'Doctor's pills, boy. He told me don't smoke no weed.'

'Weed is a natural thing.'

Hurly nodded vigorously and puffed away at the spliff. Then he passed it back to Kwate.

Edwina was looking at him, waiting for him to pass it to her in some acknowledgement of their earlier encounter. As she looked, she saw the pupils of his eyes make a slow motion upwards and his shoulders droop under their own weight and she watched his knees give way, twisting around each other.

Hurly collapsed to the floor in a heap. Suddenly there was a clearing. 'Give the man air,' someone said.

'Man drop this day here with Kenny sounds,' a fan said.

'Whose weed kill this man?' a genuinely curious voice asked above the chorus of laughter and concern.

Edwina watched Kwate lean over Hurly and touch his forehead. Kwate took charge of the situation and shifted the people who had crowded round, craning their necks for a look. He ordered somebody to move Hurly and hands lifted the boy and spaces cleared before his curt commands.

'Call a cab,' Kwate said to the vicar at the door.

'I'm afraid there's no phone here. Take him out to

the main road, there's bound to be something there.'

They dragged Hurly, still unconscious, to the main road two streets down. Edwina counted four cabs that passed them without stopping.

'Poison reach the boy,' Slingo said.

The taxi dropped Edwina and Rupert first. In the dark of the cab, with Hurly still almost unconscious lying with his head on Kwate's lap, Edwina reached out to hold Rupert's hand. He refused her hand but turned his face to her. He wanted to convey that he had simply followed her through her wilful adventure, he hadn't taken any part in it. He had watched her at the blues. She seemed electrified to be stepping on what she took to be new ground but he knew to be quicksand.

He could see her eyes shining. There was something about white features, about the expressions on white people's faces, Rupert thought, that was a shadow of the decrepitude of age. In the very boldness of her cheekbones, in the very health of her pink-veined skin, he felt he could see the metalled wrinkles of her old age. In one way she was like his mother: a girl with abandon and adventure who must have taken his father for what he was – whatever he was; Rupert didn't know. In another sense, she wasn't. His mother was an Irish woman who still believed that God, if not the Pope, would one day redeem the wickedness that life had taught Rupert. His mother was a woman of hope and optimism, whereas Edwina was not. Edwina, he felt, was content to live for the moment, and would trade whatever attractions she had for the intensity of that moment. That was why she loved, or had loved, Michael. There was no denying, Rupert thought, that Michael must, at one time, have fascinated Edwina completely, held her attention to the exclusion of all else. He could see Michael's appeal. Michael could hypnotise people into believing that their rotten little problems with their mums and dads and their quarrels on Thursday night, or their wrangles with the officials of the tenants' association, were the most important issues in the life and vitality of the country. Michael was a man for people with problems.

Just now Edwina seemed to be all attention to Slingo. Rupert could see that Slingo had been throwing words her way, and she was listening.

As they went up to his room, he was sullen.

'What's the matter, baby?' she said.

'Don't try and imitate the black girls; you'll never make it,' Rupert replied.

'You don't like mixing your friends, do you . . . Rupert?'

'You want to see the blues, you see it.'

'You haven't answered my question, darling.'

'They ain't my friends,' Rupert said, and they walked through his door to his bed.

Seven

Kwate and Slingo dumped Hurly on the doorstep of his mother's house.

'You got space, boy, space. I need a lickle space,' Hurly said, as they stood him upright. 'Boy, I feel bad.' He didn't want to face his mother in her tattered night-gown, shouting after him as he pulled the blanket over his head. He knew that Kwate and Slingo were 'big boys'; they would probably go back to the blues or move on to some other scene, talking and smoking the night out while he, with his unseasoned head, had to bear the giddiness and the sickness and the sharp tongue of a mother who understood only too well, but had too many worries of her own to sympathise. She didn't approve of Kwate, even though he made an effort to sympathise with her load. Slingo was banned from the house.

'You is still a boy, and you thinks you is man,' his mother would say.

'Man walk in righteousness, because I and I is the king of kings, lord of lords, conquering lion of the tribe of Judah,' he would answer, pouring the milk onto his cornflakes as she watched, knowing that it would succeed in teasing her.

'Go away with that stupidness,' she would say, knowing that he was not going to go away with it. He was her boy, and the sweat of her brow had given him a shelter he was forced to accept and be grateful for.

They fought over money.

'Tcha, I want my pocket money, Mum.'

'Every week you come for pocket money. Every single week, like you was a living calendar. Sometime it have two Fridays in the week. Is you workin' for it, or me?'

'Ah, tcha, Mum, throw me a two poun'.'

'And don't bother come back for no more.'

Off to club and spend it.

Saturday now. No money. Knock-knock-knock-knock. Saturday heating up.

'Hey, Hurlington dread. Shaka down the bottom of the road. Fifty pence to go in.'

'Hah, hmmmm. Hey, Mum, forward a fifty pence, nuh?'

'No. Go to bed, it pay you better. I give you two pound yesterday, no have no more. Progeny is God's leech.'

She learn a lot o' rubbish in church from white preacher.

'All right. All right, Mum. You see what I can do. I make to steal it. Jus' knock over this man, take his money, ain't it?'

Whop, tish, gone.

Heavy panting.

'Thief, thief, thief!'

Fifty pence to hand over. *Tooph do do do do do do do; Tooph do do do do do. Eeeeeeeeeeeee . . . . on; eeeeee . . . . . on; eeeeeeee . . . on.*

'All right, you. We saw you. Is this the man who mugged you?'

'Yes, it's him, it's him.'

'Right, get him, lads.' *OOOOOOOOOOOOOOOOH – ffffffff . . . . . Ring ring. Ring ring. Ring ring.* 'Hello?'

'Your son is down Kennington Police Station. He

mugged a man. Could you come down and retrieve
him ?'

'What?'

'Your son mugged this man, he'll be going to court.'

'I give my son all the money he need! He has never
needed to come and ask for money I don't give him. He
had no need to steal.'

Never any need to steal.

She will swear to lies before the magistrate, Hurly
thinks. He can smile. On his face a plastered grin, the
eternal golliwog. 'Jam jar coon,' the kids at school used
to say.

'Sit up, young man, you are not a gentleman of leisure.
You are on trial here and this is an extremely grave
offence. I have the deepest sympathy for your mother
who has, unaided, attempted to bring you up. I believe
every word of this honest lady. She has apparently
stood by you. You have given your mother endless
trouble, young man. The social report clearly shows that
you were unenthusiastic at your school, and unenthusiastic about finding suitable employment.'

'He keep bad company, the boy. Rasta man, bad.
Kwate, Black Power trouble. Slingo, which ain't the
name his respectable parents give the boy, is thief.'

*Mum you must forward into new kind of views. This
is backward thinking. To you my friends are wrong
men. Doesn't matter what, they are wrong. They're
nasty. They don't wash their hair . . . no matter if they
do, they are Rasta and they're wrong. We're not supposed to associate with them. We're not supposed to go
to sound system because a whole heap of black people*

*together is bound to cause trouble. It's bad company we
keeping up.*

'You read *Daily Mirror* it makes your brain soft.'

'Black people is bad company.'

One or two friends come round my house. 'Mind them
don't thief up me something, you know.'

'Mother, they wouldn't do that.'

Next morning. 'Hurlington, where me ten pound . . .
what ! . . . me rent money gone.'

'There it is for you. I never stole it, Mum.'

'Don't bring in them friend again, them too thief.

'All right, Mother, I'll dissociate myself from them,
I'm going to turn white.'

'Don't do that, you can't do that. If you come in house
with white woman, you nah come in here again. Kick
out.'

A man who is by himself will pay better.

'Mum, I don't know what to do. Can't go with white
people, can't go with black people, what am I supposed
to do, Mum?'

Them say, 'the sweet nanny goat go bitter'. 'What you
want out in them world with black people, you going
get it.'

'Yeh, Mum, I want a whole heap of money.'

'And you goin' thief it.'

'All right, Mum, leave it, jus' leave it.'

Eight

After the night at the blues, Edwina established herself at Rupert's. That contact with a forbidden world, forbidden by her upbringing and by Rupert, had excited her. She referred to her own place as 'Michael's flat', going back there only to pick up a pair of curtains or a bed-cover or an LP that she remembered and said she didn't want to live without. Slowly she was taking over. She painted the walls of Rupert's room, she bought a desk and sanded it and varnished it and piled it with her books and her school work.

Rupert would wait for her to return from school. He liked having her clothes hanging up in the wall cupboard, he liked the smell of her, her natural perfume reminding him of the charm that he had won. He hadn't returned to the drama group after the night of Michael's confession. He knew he couldn't face Michael. It would be like facing a man who deserved what you had taken from him. He felt confused. Sure, he'd won Edwina away, he wanted her, but he didn't want her now in the way she gave herself. He wanted her to belong to him and yet to not be there. It seemed to him that she had stopped giving him her seriousness now that she had given him herself. She didn't talk to him in the way she used to.

He was proud that the rest of them, Hurly and all, looked upon her as 'his woman'. He wouldn't say that in her presence. She objected to that sort of phrase; she was no one's woman, no one's wife, no one's girl, she said. She said that what mattered to her was the feeling of not being tied down. She said that women were just like blacks, and though Rupert thought she was wrong, he didn't say so. It would cause her to argue and she always won arguments, she was better at words than he was, but she was still wrong. It made him smile when she compared herself to his mother. 'Your mum has put up a struggle all her life. It's difficult enough for a white woman who takes up with blacks now, but think of what it was like twenty years ago.' She would talk to him about the prejudice that his mother must have had to put up with, and Rupert would listen. In his heart of hearts he knew that his mother was not like that.

She never thought like Edwina. She had just done what she had to, what she wanted to, she wasn't on no crusade.

On Tuesday nights Edwina still went to the drama club. Rupert knew that it was where her seriousness would be given free rein. She knew about drama, she knew about young people, she would pose, posture, make them want to imitate her. He didn't want her to go. 'Rupert, you aren't jealous of Michael?' she would say. She'd smile and then frown and immediately reassure him.

'It's all kid stuff,' he would say.

'You're kid stuff,' she would reply. 'It's my work. I've known Michael so many years. We can do things together without the feeling of doing them together, you know what I mean?'

But Rupert would sulk.

Edwina didn't like Rupert's possessive moods. She

didn't like the way he glared at her when she talked to Slingo or to Kwate or the other boys that came there. Kwate fascinated her. All of them, even Rupert in a strange way, gave off an air of challenge. They were not like white men, Edwina thought. They wouldn't make it clear in any way that they fancied you, and yet they'd set themselves up as targets of attraction.

In Kwate, she felt, there was an extreme self-consciousness about every move, every gesture that he made in front of her. He had a way of summing up the faces and people before him, just as Michael had the knack of adding up facts that made an argument. Both Michael and Kwate were wary of being cheated, but Michael was wary of opinions and arguments and people's mentalities and interests. Kwate seemed to be wary of people as they presented themselves, of the pretences that people put forward for other people to see. And yet he was a pretender himself.

He flattered her. After the night at the blues she met him again in the house. He didn't give her the attention she wanted as they sat around Slingo's room, but he turned to her when Rupert had gone out of the room to make some coffee and suddenly said, 'You must have done some modelling.'

'No,' she said.

'Naw, I just thought from the way you sit. You look like you was one of the gel I saw in the TV ads.'

When Rupert came back into the room, Kwate abruptly stopped talking to her. There was a recognition in this circle, she thought, that she belonged to him, and Edwina felt instinctively that she wanted to defy it.

Being around that house, she picked up phrases from Slingo and Kwate, and used them with her drama classes in school, to the delight of all the black kids. She would refer to money as 'breads' or 'donzai'; she would use the words of reggae lyrics as though they were proverbs. 'Who the cap fit, let them wear it,' she would say, or, 'Those who deal in violence, shall go in silence,' and the black boys in her fifth form would say, 'Where you get that from, miss?' She knew that it was whispered around the class that she went with a lot of black men. She liked conveying that impression. It gave her a sense of power.

Rupert didn't like her adopting the phrases and language of the ghetto.

'You do it yourself. It's just as much a bluff for you as for me,' she would argue.

'You make yourself out like white trash. Like the girls who hang around black clubs looking for a bit of black.'

'Don't ever talk to *me* in that way!' She was terrified that there might be some truth in Rupert's accusation. She knew that in speech she insisted on talking about black people, white people, anybody, as though they were the same, knowing that in reality there was a world of difference between them. She had learnt, especially through Kwate, that she must not try to deny or abandon her 'whiteness'. Before him or Slingo, she was always careful to preserve her accent and the cast of mind that contact with them seemed to be warping.

But by degrees she discovered that Rupert wasn't what she had wanted him to be. She hadn't bothered to disguise her affair with him in the drama group, because she thought she saw in him a kind of wildness which she wanted, needed like a medicine. She could now see, after virtually living with him for a month, that he was confused and frightened and directionless.

One Tuesday night she got to Rupert's room from work and found that he wasn't waiting for her. She had decided she would go to the drama workshop that night and had spoken to Michael on the phone from school. He had been distinctly cool, giving her the impression that she wasn't welcome there, and it worried her. She had expected him to want to see her. When Rupert came in, she told him that she was leaving at seven.

He didn't reply.

'What's the matter? Why are you being childish again?'

'Why don't you go back to Michael if it's him you want to see all the time.'

'Don't exaggerate. I haven't seen him for weeks, and I want to see the girls at the drama club.'

'You think I'm too stupid for you, don't you, just because I can't read you all that poetry and talk about Shakespeare.'

'I only think you're stupid when you throw these jealous fits.'

Rupert stormed out. 'Go where you want,' he shouted, 'and don't bother to come back!'

She had felt the edge of his temper. Too sharp, she thought. When he'd gone, she tidied up his room, folding his clothes. She'd have to wait for him to come back, she decided. She wouldn't go to the drama club. She'd be there when he got back and tell him so.

That evening Kwate knocked on the door and came into Rupert's room. It was obvious that Slingo had told him that there had been a row.

'The boy leave you?' he asked.

'Rupert's just gone out for a bit, he should be back.' She smiled. She was lying on the bed reading.

'Is you I want to talk to,' Kwate said.

'Oh?'

'Slingo must have told you about the film?'

'He said something weeks ago, but I'm not going to drama any more and I don't suppose we can do it.'

'I want to talk to you about being photographed,' Kwate said.

'What do you mean photographed?'

'You know in m'camera a click and "say cheese"?'

Kwate was so easy with her. It was a new side to him. Edwina wanted to talk to him, had wanted the opportunity before, but now Rupert might be coming back any moment.

Kwate sensed her discomfort. 'You got a car, ain't you?' he asked.

'Why?'

'I thought me and you could go out and have a drink and maybe talk about it?'

'You mean now?'

'Why not?' He said it with supreme self-assurance, knowing she'd agree.

He asked her to drive out of Brixton, south towards Blackheath.

'Why don't we go somewhere closer?' She knew the answer. He was taking her where he wouldn't be seen with her by people he knew.

'I don't like drink in Brixton,' he said.

He drank about six barley wines and seemed unaffected by them. Edwina tried to keep up with his drinking and with the quick conversation he made. She drove Kwate home, a few streets down from Rupert's place, and he asked her up. She parked the car in a dark little side street without explaining to Kwate why. She followed him up the unlit stairs, three storeys up to his room.

On the wall there were posters, one about Freedom Fighters in Angola and another depicting a black man chained to a Nazi cross, fighting a fist loose from his chains and holding it up in a salute, with a tremendous strain of Promethean muscle. There were drawings on the wall that Kwate had done himself, of rasta men with their hair in waterfalls, their beards fanning out into mountain ranges.

Edwina stood before the pictures.

'What do you do apart from painting and photography?'

'I'm a poet.'

She smiled, but checked herself when she saw that he was quite serious and that his bony cheeks and slightly slanting Chinese eyes were imposing that seriousness on her.

'Can I see what you've written?'

'Man could be a poet and not write nothing.'

'I think these drawings are beautiful,' she said.

'You could see them better if you lie back on the bed,' he said.

She found herself willing to play this game. He sat in the middle of the floor and rolled a spliff. He put on a Marvin Gaye LP on the record player. His head looked defiant in the dim light. It was flattering the way he strutted about just for her. He hadn't talked about his and Slingo's films or his photography all evening. He'd talked about white people and black people and his contempt for people who didn't know where they were at, like hippies and like the girls who hung around blacks. He was talking to her about it so he must exclude her from that category, she thought.

78

She stayed the night in Kwate's room.

The next day Rupert asked her how the drama club had gone. He was sorry for having walked out on her, he said.

'It was all right, just the usual, and you don't have to apologise, I should be sorry. I push you too much. You were right: Michael plods on with his drama and his group, but he doesn't really know where it's at.'

'Man must feel the pain,' Rupert said.

Edwina was used to men looking at her possessively. Michael looked at her as though he'd lost a battle but would win the war. Rupert had the look of a young boy with his first mechanical toy. When Kwate glanced at her, his glance said that he could command what he didn't care to possess, and when he stared at her, he seemed to be saying that he could shape and mould anything that was uncertain and unformed when he took it in his hands.

Nine

The second deadline comes and goes. Chief Superintendent Burgess is almost certain that the gunmen he has on his hands are not willing to shoot any one of their hostages. The Metropolitan Police Commissioner has taken charge of the over-all strategy of the siege and the Home Secretary calls a conference of psychiatrists, the social workers who will give evidence to the police, and the actual men who are to implement the tactical assault on what the papers have begun to call 'The Mini-cab Siege'.

Burgess and other senior officers are of the opinion that the gunmen should be given assurances that they will be allowed onto a plane and out of the country, and they argue for trapping the three on the open tarmac of the airport. If they can be brought out into the open, they can be shot. They submit a detailed plan for such an operation.

The plan is vetoed, as P.C. Bully tells his colleagues, 'by the Big Boy himself'. There is little doubt that the plan would work, a very low probability that the hostages would get shot into the bargain, but the Home Office says that it prefers the law-breakers to be brought to justice alive. Burgess argues for a speedy conclusion. The Commissioner, having heard the arguments, decrees that the alternative strategy be tried.

Outside the siege, unbeknown to the seven people inside, there have been certain incidents. Three hundred police with horses, vans and batons, have stopped a crowd of about a hundred young black people marching towards the scene of the siege. The incident goes unreported in the national press, but the small newspapers were there and have plastered the black ghettoes of the country with posters demanding 'An End to the Frustration of the Black Masses'. This propaganda, tied as it is to current gossip in the pubs and market places of London, has something to do with the Commissioner's decision. 'He's in a dead funk about the niggers,' P.C. Bully says, and one of the young officers at his station says, 'I think the guv's right, we'd have a bloody riot if the coons were shot.'

'Kwate's a sly one,' Bully says, enjoying the notoriety which his professional acquaintance with one of the gunmen gives him. 'He hasn't the liquid gumption to do the hostages.'

The hostages have all been sent their own clothes, a way of telling them that the police are in close contact with their relatives. The three black men are sent jeans and T-shirts and three pairs of pants and socks. Hurly notices that the police have sent two size thirties and one size thirty-four, the first two presumably for Kwate and Rupert and the last for him. They fit perfectly, uncannily well, as though the police have identikit descriptions of each of them.

Inside the musty room, the change of clothes comes as an occasion. They have spent the last night and day playing cards, all except Kwate who sits sullenly outside the circle. With the change of clothes, Kwate allows each of the hostages to have a thorough wash, leaving the door to the kitchen open and supervising them himself. The girl goes in last. Kwate jerks his head to indicate to Hurly that he wants him to take charge of her.

Kwate goes over and sits by the window and begins unloading the bullets from the pockets of his leather jacket. The Greek man and the child stare at the bullets and look away, as though embarrassed.

When Kwate sleeps, and they are left in the hands of Rupert and Hurly, the hostages carry on conversations with them. The guns are put away, left lying around. Rupert is convinced that none of the four will try to make a dash for the door. He can see that neither the boy nor his father will try anything without the other, and that the girl seems to do only what the white man approves. He keeps his eye on the man, certain that he can tackle him, even without a gun, almost wishing that he'd make some move and turn this waiting relationship into a physical scrap.

The girl washes her hair.

'Your hair look nice now, eh?' Hurly says as they come into the room.

'You use up all the Fairy?' Kwate demands, looking up from his fiddling with the shotgun.

She looks startled. 'I used some. I think there's some left.'

'You let her use it?' Kwate asks Hurly. There is a hint of frustration in his voice.

'Tcha, leave me alone,' Hurly says.

'And you want gamble with this man here because you think I don't know?'

The previous night, as Kwate slept, Hurly played flush with the white man for money.

There is a tense, dispirited silence in the room.

'Just passing time,' Hurly says.

'You'll be doing time, not passing it,' Kwate says.

'You can't see this man here taking you for a slow ride and you too fool to have any understanding of it.'

'Leave it.' Hurly says.

'I feel like leaving all you,' Kwate says.

'Why don't you go then? Nobody holding a gun in your mouth.'

'I didn't want to start this,' the girl says. 'He couldn't see what I was doing; I needed to wash my hair.'

'I was checking her careful,' Hurly protests.

Kwate thrusts a bullet into the chamber of the shotgun. 'Teach me not to play with little boys.'

'You is a big boy, you should play with the police.'

'You're like a couple of clowns,' Rupert interrupts.

Kwate and Hurly are instantly silent. Hurly pretends that he is tidying up the room and busies himself with picking up the clothes that they've thrown all round the room. Nobody speaks for half an hour. It is obvious to Rupert that the hostages are frightened every time an argument breaks out between one of them and Kwate.

'How much money you take off him in the poker?' Kwate asks, not looking at Hurly.

'Two thousand pound.'

'You ain't going to get a chance to spend it in a wooden box.'

'You'll be wearing some plank yourself,' Hurly replies.

'You two should go on the box, better than the Fosters,' says Rupert.

'We *going* to be on telly,' Kwate says.

Hurly doesn't pick up the remark, but Rupert can see that Kwate is anxious to end the bickering.

'How you mean?'

Kwate isn't going to explain straight away. He waits till their consignment of food arrives. He does not allow anyone to touch anything.

83

'Get a pen,' he says to Rupert. Then he goes over to the Greek man. 'You could write English, couldn't yuh?'

The man nods.

'Write this note.'

The man takes up the pen.

'*Calling Burgess*,' Kwate dictates. '*We are taking no food until you give us a proper television set*. Write that down.'

'Why you don't just ask Burgess straight?' Hurly asks, unable to contain his curiosity. Kwate does not answer.

The Greek writes the note. Kwate puts it on the tray full of sandwiches and hands the tray to Rupert.

'Put it out in the corridor.'

'I want eat,' Rupert says.

'Put it in the corridor.'

Rupert does as he is told.

Kwate goes to the window and, standing behind the curtain, shouts to the street below: 'Burgess! Come and get your tray and your sandwich!'

Kwate has taken charge once again, but Hurly is still smouldering.

No food is sent up the whole of the next day. Hurly sleeps and Rupert follows him. When Rupert wakes up, Kwate and Hurly seem to be on speaking terms. Kwate is lecturing. He is aware that the hostages are listening to each word, weighing it up for the force of personality behind it rather than for the meaning.

'If we are free, we have to be free together. We have pose a problem for your mother and others like her, boy. They now have to stand up and be counted. I sure the government count them, and when they see that we are all in numbers, black people of the whole world, then it terrorise their mind. We have to rely on the com-

84

munity and know what they are doing. It doesn't matter what happens to us, the fight have to go on. . . .'

It is Kwate's turn to sleep after Rupert. Rupert makes sure that he is asleep before he motions to Hurly and walks to the kitchen to fetch the biscuits that have been put back there. He hands the hostages a fair share of the packet and he and Hurly begin to eat, casting an eye from time to time on Kwate's form, covered over with a blanket.

'How much days you think we got?' Hurly asks.

Rupert raises his hand to his lips to tell him to shut up.

'I want some coffee.'

When Rupert comes back from the kitchen with the mugs he can see that there is something wrong with the Greek man. He is slouched against the wall behind the settee and his face has gone grey. His moustaches hang down, looking sad, and his large eyes seem full of involuntary pleading.

They sit drinking the coffee in silence. The Greek man begins panting like a dog after a chase, and the sound of his breath, pulled through his open mouth, turns everyone's eyes to him. His eyes roll back and his lungs seem to strain for air.

The boy rushes to his father and starts clawing at his shirt and undoing the belt on his trousers.

'Attack,' he says to Hurly, not caring if he wakes Kwate. 'Must get a doctor, right away, please.'

'He's having a fit,' the girl says, and her voice awakens Kwate who throws the blanket off his head and sits bolt upright, holding the shotgun.

The Greek man has now sunk onto the settee, his legs sprawled out. He is holding his chest with both hands.

Tears trickle out of his eyes and he holds out one of his palms to motion Hurly away. Hurly dashes to the window and draws the curtains back.

'Get him to some fresh air,' the white man shouts, following Hurly's cue, and he rushes to the Greek man and begins pulling the settee towards the window.

Kwate leaps up and switches off the light, plunging the room in darkness.

'What go on?' he shouts.

'This man dying.'

'What you done to him?'

'Is *you* stop his food.'

Kwate pushes the white man and Hurly aside. By the light of the street-lamp which comes through the window, he examines his eyes.

'He's had a heart attack,' the white man says.

'You a doctor?' Kwate turns on him.

The Greek man's body lies like a machine, gasping for air.

'It's true, his heart faint,' Hurly says putting his head to the man's chest.

'Call the bloody ambulance. Call the police, they'll get him out of here,' the white man says.

Kwate turns on him and pushes the gun into his chest. The man backs away.

'Oh no,' the white girl begins to scream.

Rupert throws himself in between Kwate and the white man. Even in the dark he can see Kwate's eyes flashing, and for an instant Rupert believes that Kwate is capable of killing a man.

Hurly pushes his head outside the window and shouts for Burgess. The policemen in the street rush into the doorway of the building, and Bully's voice comes faintly down the corridor.

'Put that down, man, put it down,' Rupert begs Kwate. The white man stands with his hands in the air against the wall.

'I'll blast your head off,' Kwate says over Rupert's shoulder. 'You think you're smart, but I'll carry you with me.'

Once again camera bulbs begin flashing in the dark outside.

Kwate reaches for Rupert's shoulder and pulls him down, the shotgun still trained on the white man.

'We want to get a man out! Man dying!' Hurly is screaming through the window. Kwate makes a deft movement towards him and pulls him down by the leg.

'What's going on?' says Burgess's level voice.

'The Greek man, you could take him, get him out of here,' Hurly shouts desperately over the sill. 'He's sick or something, he need doctor.'

Burgess takes a second to consider the implication in the statement.

'We'll send a stretcher up.'

Kwate relaxes slightly and nods. Rupert can see that Kwate didn't quite know what to do, but has regained his calculating balance.

In the street there is an ambulance standing by. In a moment two men come up the stairs and down the corridor.

'We're coming through, we're ambulance men.'

'Is all right, Rupert?' Kwate asks. His voice betrays anxiety. He crawls over to the boy who has thrown himself across his father, fanning him ineffectively and crying. He pulls the boy off with a tremendous struggle and drags him across the floor to the kitchen.

'You killed him!' the boy shouts.

'I'm letting them through,' Rupert says, his voice raised unnecessarily.

The men bearing the stretcher don't look in the least intimidated. They go straight over to the Greek man and pile his unconscious body on the stretcher.

'Can we call through the window, mate? Who's in charge here?' one of them asks, looking round the darkened room as he kneels by the Greek.

'Just get him out,' Hurly says, training his pistol on the white man who is still standing with his hands absurdly aloft.

'Get him downstairs,' Rupert commands, standing at the door.

From the kitchen the boy screams and Rupert can hear Kwate slapping him. The boy shouts in a combination of Greek and English and Kwate growls at him. The boy begins to sob. None of the others move. The stretcher-bearers behave all through as though it is not their business, or at least that's what the routine movements of their bodies imply. They hurry through the door, taking small mincing steps, loaded with the weight of the Greek man.

Kwate pokes his head through the kitchen door and the rest of them can see that he is holding down the boy with his left hand. For the first time his expression is one of genuine uncertainty. 'Keep your eye on the boy,' he says to Rupert and his accent is amazingly English.

He goes up to the window and peers out. The ambulance has driven up to the door. Kwate turns and trains his shotgun on the door to the corridor. He is desperate to show the others that everything is under control.

'Sit against the wall,' he says to the white man and motions the girl to sit next to him.

Burgess's voice comes over the loud-hailer after the ambulance has gone. 'You'd better send the young boy down now. We want you to surrender one of the hostages.'

'Send us a telly and we'll send him down,' Kwate shouts back. The police want him to repeat it. Kwate does.

'All right, we'll send you a telly; send the boy down.'

'We can wait.'

'Kwate, are you listening? So can we!'

Kwate turns to Rupert and asks him to bring the boy to the window. The boy is silent now, shepherded under escort. He licks his lips like a whipped puppy and he looks at Kwate with hatred. Kwate seems to change his mind and motions to Rupert to send the boy to sit next to the others.

'You could go soon,' Hurly says to the boy, who refuses to sit, but stands defiantly against the wall.

An hour later the television set arrives. It is placed, according to Kwate's instructions, at the end of the corridor. Rupert drags it in while Kwate stands over him with a weapon to cover his return.

'So let the boy go,' Hurly says.

'You gone mad or something?' Kwate asks. 'The boy ain't going nowhere.'

Ten

The television set is on all day. Kwate has turned the sound down. He doesn't look at the box. The others sit, glancing now and then at the silently moving image. The boy sits with his elbows between his knees and the girl talks to him in whispers. He nods or shakes his head every now and then. Hurly resumes his card game with the white man.

Rupert is despondent. He is thinking: We'll never get out of here. All of them, three hostages, three captors, are aware that the television set gives them a possibility of one-sided speech with an organised world outside.

At five forty-five, Kwate twists his body on the floor and turns up the sound.

The siege of the mini-cab office enters its sixth day. Police report that they have supplied the three gunmen with a television set. The condition of the hostage released yesterday, fifty-three-year-old Georgias Photopoulos, manager of the car firm, remains critical. In what is referred to as a major breakthrough, the fourth man in the robbery and ransom plan was apprehended in a flat in South London earlier today and has been charged. The names of the three gunmen are now known to be Rupert Dowling, aged nineteen, Aloysius Brown, aged twenty-eight, and Hurlington Macaulay, aged twenty-two, all of South London. Chief Superintendent Burgess, in charge of operations at the scene of the siege in Corbett Street in London's West End, said that

several people are helping police with their enquiries.
Earlier, the gunmen agreed to release a second hostage,
twelve-year-old Panos Photopoulos, but they failed to
deliver him when negotiations between them and the
police broke down. Several MPs have welcomed the
Home Secretary's statement that there will be no surren-
der in this country to terrorism of any sort.

Kwate turns the set off and paces the room.

'They lie.' he says through his clenched teeth.

The boy knew the names of the white kids, and the
name of the dog. They would parade it around on its
leash even in the central square where it wouldn't be
killed in the traffic. When they let it off the leash the
black kids would gather round it and stroke it and throw
sticks for it to fetch, until the dog had to go home when
their daddy called the kids in.

Hurly remembers how the boy longed to own a dog
himself and train it to ferocity, to protect him from his
enemies. His yellow dog, he was sure from the first,
couldn't be taught to do any of that. It was a ridiculous
dog. He couldn't even stop it from straining at the string,
rushing nose-first to the garbage cans when he took it
into the street. In a week the puppy grew thinner and
began to lose its hair. His dad, when he came home,
would spank it off the chairs and kick it into the corner.
His mum fed it, now and then, with scraps from their
own meals.

The boy tried taking it for walks as the white kids
took their dog, and found that Tiger had to be dragged
most of the way. He learnt that the cur had a mind of
its own, living on a wave-length of smells, poking its
head through the parapet bars of basements on the way,
magnetised by all the filth it encountered, blandly un-

aware of the commands that the boy barked when other people were looking.

One day, on one of these dragging walks, an old white lady crossed the road and called out to the boy, 'Where are you dragging that dog?'

'It's my dog,' the boy said.

'We are all God's creatures,' she said, 'and it's not your dog at all.'

'My dad bought it.'

The old white lady bent down and stroked the dog's head firmly, stretching the circles of its eyes. 'They don't feed you too well, do they, my lovely? They've starved my little thing. Oh, look at the state of you, poor doggy.'

The boy dragged the dog away from under her hand, and holding the string tight, began to run. She shouted out something after him, but he didn't hear. There were tears in his eyes. He knew that they didn't feed it enough. He hadn't wanted it to live as a tottering skeleton.

He went home and told his mother, 'The dog must have the tins we see on the telly.'

'You speaking to the dog now?'

'I tell you he's very sick.'

'I never want the beast in my house. I go tell the man take it away before it fill its belly with my everything.'

When his dad came that night, the boy saw he was drunk. There was a terrible row, and the boy knew it was over the dog, because he heard his mum say that one beast was too many for the house, and his dad struck her. The boy knew that some blows were going to reach him, too. As his dad came for the dog in a rage and carried it out, staggering with the struggling pup under his arm, the boy tried to hold him back and joined in the general shouting. His mother was crying.

His dad banged the door behind him with a curse and his mum clung to the boy, partly to pacify him, partly to console herself.

The next morning the children gathered in the square around the pile of old furniture, gutted mattresses and eviscerated TV sets, staring at the fly-infested body of the yellow puppy. The boy had taken one horrified look and dashed back into the house calling his mum. His mother saw the terror in his face and came out with him into the square and stood before all the willing stares of the neighbours, shouting, 'The filthy dog break the boy's heart,' which they all knew referred not to the yellow dog, but to the boy's father.

The children in the square were too amazed to laugh. Days later they told the boy that the puppy had been battered to death with a brick from the building rubble outside the posh houses. The boy wouldn't go out and play. The shame had cut him; he felt the derision and pity of the other children and their mothers. They knew. Life had so many open windows without curtains. That was the beginning of his wish to be away from there, to go and live in a house such as the old white lady must have had, and buy the proper dog food from the supermarket.

His dad had committed murder, but didn't act like a man who had. He came home a few days after and without the least exchange of words his mother settled down to cooking him a meal and to drinking rum with him. His dad brought the boy some comics, Hurly remembers, and he spent the next few days staring at them, turning their pages, lounging on the carpet or sitting at the kitchen table. 'The boy fond of reading,' his mum said.

*   *

Hurly remembers the school and Mr McSweeney with the thick curly hair and the sticking-out ears. The other kids called him 'Big Ears'. He taught them English and paced up and down the class while he talked, like a clockwork lion in the cartoons.

He would sometimes say to the boy, 'The Queen's English is not the English of the jungle, and it can't be wrote that way.' The class had been trained to laugh dutifully at his jokes, and they did it with a mixture of delight and contempt. He used to call kids to his desk, seat them next to him and go through their books with a thick red pencil making sarcastic remarks. Big Ears was funny: jovial on the outside, but when the boy stood next to him, able to smell his heavy breath, he knew there was more to Mr McSweeney's sarcasm than the desire to be funny.

He filled the boy with a kind of fear. Hurly remembers that he hated him.

He gave a lesson once on 'Negro English'. 'What is a young black baby called?' he asked the class.

'*A little nigger.*'

'*A jam jar label.*'

'*We can only be sure if we are sensitive.*'

'It's called a piccaninny,' he announced when no one answered.

'That's mustard stuff sir,' a girl said.

The class laughed and McSweeney seemed well pleased.

'What does your mother refer to you as, Hurly? Not as her little blue-eyed boy, hmm?'

'She calls me Hurly, sir.'

'The word is piccaninny. Come on, you must have heard it, hmmm?'

'No, sir.'

94

'What is it, what's the word, Janice?'

'Piccadilly, sir.'

He told his mother about the lesson. She didn't take any notice, but when his dad next appeared she said, 'They teaching this child all kind of rubbish in that school you put him.'

'Mr McSweeney taught us some Negro English today. He said all black boys were called Piccadilly.'

'Who tell you that thing?'

'Mr McSweeney.'

'What he is? Is he Irish?'

'That headmaster too fool, calling on paddy man to teach English.'

'He says we speak like the jungle.'

'Kick him on his knee,' his dad said, visibly annoyed. Hurly was glad of it.

'Send him back to Dublin and tell him take his nasty potato back with him,' his dad said. He rose from the table and picked up a potato from the vegetable bucket and gave it to Hurly.

His mum laughed. 'Say your dad give him his wages.'

The next morning on the way to school, Hurly remembered the potato. He slipped it into a paper bag, excited by the idea of getting a laugh out of the others.

He gave it to Mr McSweeney as soon as the lesson began and the class was coming into the English room and taking their places. Big Ears pulled the potato out of the paper bag.

'My dad sent you extra wages,' Hurly ventured.

The kids tittered but stopped when they saw the face between the ears turned red. It was as Hurly had suspected. Big Ears could dish it out, but he couldn't take it.

McSweeney threw the potato into the bin without a

word and after class called Hurly over to his desk, ordering the rest of the children to clear out of his room.

Thirty-five-year-old McSweeney confronted twelve-
year-old Hurly across the desk. His eyes glinted and his
mouth was turned ever so slightly down at the corners.

'Never play those games with me, little boy. Never
again make any jokes about anyone's race. You can't
make a fool of me, the Almighty has done that already.
But I, my lad, I could make a cripple of you.'

The edge in his voice told Hurly that these words he
should not remember or repeat. Not to his dad, not to
the others who would definitely ask what Big Ears had
said and done.

The threat made Hurly swallow hard. 'No, sir.'

Some days later McSweeney, his jovial mood restored,
asked the class, 'Why do you think the Irishman put a
lock on his trouser zip? To stop people taking the piss.

The class laughed. Hurly didn't. He looked away from
the teacher when he saw his eyes turn to him in the
third row. After class McSweeney turned to Hurly on
his way out.

'I see we understand each other perfectly,' he said.

Hurly remembers the boy, confused at the ripe age
of sixteen, wanting to imitate the limp that the 'rude
boys', the 'Johnny-too-bads' of Brixton affected. They
called him the 'lame-dance boy'.

He remembers the boy learning from his associates to
give off confidence like a body smell. He remembers his
first encounter with Kwate.

He went now where the other black boys went. He
heard of a gang called the Rebels, and in his dreams he
wanted to join them, but the Rebels were nowhere to
be found. Everyone talked about them. They struck here,

they attacked there. There were many stories, but no people, no faces to fit into the stories. The Rebels were bad! Badder! Baddest! They'd robbed a whole super-market, they'd gone into Brixton nick and rescued a boy belonging to their gang, they'd set fire to a police van and still they were free and unfettered. Some of the boys he knew by name and face were reputed to be Rebels, but they weren't the people in the stories at all : they were the same rude boys, the same lame-dance men who were no smarter than he was, and as poor as he was.

'There ain't no Rebels, boy, *you* is the Rebels,' Kwate told him.

'You don't know what the Rebels do,' Hurly said.

'I know what they do. They get on bus and don't pay ticket, that's what they do,' Kwate said.

He met Kwate at the fair. He had gone to Brockwell Park with a crowd of boys from the youth club. It was summer. The sun was shining so that you could wear your shirt open as they do in Jamaican films, sweating, shining. They had come down to the Park to listen to the music at the festival. But the music at the festival was no good. The sound, amplified and pumped through twenty boxes, faded away into the clear sky. It was not a sound of freedom, it was a sound that needed to be enclosed in four walls, tightly packed with bodies to be effective, to deliver its mysteries. In the clear open air, it hung above the heads of the crowd and vanished. There were clowns on the platform, hundreds of boys and girls clambering on, dying to be seen. The Park was thick with policemen. In front of the platform stood an indifferent crowd. A few hundred people, mostly white people, the sort of hippy whites who live in Brixton. squatted on the grass. Hurly's gang was fed up with the sounds, fed up with the clowns who tried to make funny speeches before they tuned their guitars.

They wandered down to the stalls at the back of the mob. A white man was selling ice-creams from a painted van. He was doing hard business. One of Hurly's crowd suggested that they go and get themselves some ice-creams. There was a crowd of young blacks around the van. Hands reached out for the cones which hung above their heads. The white man wanted money in his hand before he loosed his tight grip on the ice-creams.

Suddenly there was a shout. Hurly looked up to see that several hands had grabbed the cones from the man's hand and the man was shouting for help. Two policemen rushed up and began to push their way through the crowd. Some youths shoved Hurly forward while others, retreating from the confusion, tried to push away. The white man had climbed down from his van and grabbed hold of a black youth by the collar. Hands reached for his white coat to pull him down. The policemen were in the thick of it. Helmets began to fly.

Some of Hurly's gang were now at the base of the van. It began to shudder. Hurly saw that it was being lifted and overturned. More police arrived from nowhere. Hurly wanted to get out. A blue-sleeved arm grabbed him and began to wrench him away from the crowd. He protested that he wasn't in it : it had nothing to do with him. 'I've got you,' the voice said. 'I've got you. Come here !' He was in the grip of the law.

Then just as he was being yanked to the edge of the crowd, into what he saw was a group of waiting policemen, a black palm fell like an axe on the hand that gripped his sleeve. The hand let go. Hurly was free. He looked up to see Kwate.

'Keep going,' Kwate said.

Ten youths were arrested. The police van took them away. Hurly was standing on the edge of the audience which was still digging the sounds, lazily, ignoring the occurrence round the ice-cream van, when Kwate's face loomed up again.

'Why you want to steal the man ice-cream? You so hungry?'

'I wasn't in that,' Hurly protested. Kwate smiled.

'You don't like ice-cream?' he asked.

There was no need to thank Kwate. Hurly felt that that was understood.

He met Kwate again at the youth club. Someone was trying to sell Hurly a gold watch for two pounds. Kwate sauntered up from nowhere and handled the watch. 'That's not worth two pound, it's worth two years,' he said.

Hurly recognized him. He hung around, back to the wall, talking to Kwate. A man of purpose, he felt.

Hurly remembers that the boy had wanted to be like every man who frightened him. His mother used to tell him to love his enemy, and he found he wanted to love him because it was a way of keeping 'in' with him. *Love thine enemy's power*, he used to think each time he looked at the ornate Christian motto hung on the wall of his mum's house.

Kwate changed all that. You have to be smart enough for the world, Kwate told him, not only violent enough for it. Hurly recalls striving to wrap that sense of dread about him, that cloak of mastery, a way of holding your head and speaking in the deepest tones, censoring your voice before it came out of your mouth. He had been slightly frightened by the men who hung around the corners in the market-place, passing comment on

99

the girls going by. Now he himself loitered on the very same corners; he had become one of them, preoccupied with the records one could buy from the booming shop on a Saturday if only one had the money.

From Kwate he learned that a man must have one soul in his body, that he has to choose his corner and defend it, that two styles don't live easily in the same body. But from so many around him, he did not know which style to adopt.

He remembers his first political meeting. Kwate advised him to go, but didn't go with him. He went with Slingo. It took some persuasion to get Slingo to agree to come along, but Slingo wanted to try to raise some bread.

'There'll be a whole heap of black people at the meeting,' offered Hurly.

'Where is it?'

'Down the youth club in Railton Road.'

They went. Slingo from the beginning began to look around the room to see which of the crowd might buy little packets for a pound from him after the business was done. Hurly had dressed for the occasion. He was wearing a hat and a green satin shirt with a jacket he had bought from Cecil Gee.

There were about fifty people in the room, mostly young but with a sprinkling of long-haired white men who worked in the social services in the area and were generally known but not acknowledged by the crowd.

At the front of the small hall in which the chairs were laid out as though for a church gathering, the politicos were assembled, talking to each other, and ignoring the crowd which sat in clusters, avoiding the front rows.

A half-bald man called the meeting to order. He said he was from the Black Revolutionary Action Group

(BRAG) and he'd like to welcome the brothers and sisters to the meeting on the problems of black youth. He was wearing a tatty olive-green jacket, and Hurly thought he must have bought it from the army surplus. He had startlingly wide eyes.

'Good to see so many of my brothers and sisters here tonight,' the man from BRAG said. 'Black people beginning to take the struggle seriously, boy.' His remark raised a laugh from the members of his organisation in the front row.

'Tramp,' Slingo said, refusing to sit down and leaning up against the wall with the air of having wandered in because he had five minutes to spare.

The first speaker of the evening was introduced. She was a fat young woman in her late twenties with short, close-cropped hair, wearing what Hurly called an African shirt above a pair of baggy khaki trousers. She stood up with a show of seriousness and then, without warning, gave the audience a really charming smile. She began to speak. 'Brothers and Sisters,' she said, stressing every word, 'we call this meeting because we want to speak to our own people and especially the youth who are at the forefront of the struggle today.' The front row cheered and some people further back joined in. 'The youth are fighting terrific odds in this country which some people call Great Britain. I can't see what's so great about it [cheer] when the sun don't shine half the time and a mango cost you ten bob in Brixton market [cheer of recognition].'

Hurly didn't like that kind of girl. Too much mouth to make up for lack of face, he thought. Yet he listened carefully, as did the majority of the audience. The girl talked eloquently about the suffering of black people in the canefields. Hurly learned something new. She

talked about why the police fight black youth and said –
as far as Hurly could understand – that the government
of this place was no different from the government of
the islands of the West Indies.

'We are organising,' she continued, 'but I don't intend
to tell you all how we organising, because there are a
lot of black people who are dangerous. They get a little
money so they work for the Special Branch. We serious
in this business, you know. We must criticise ourselves
for all the loose talk that we do, because black people
talk loose you know, their tongues loose like a donkey
tail.'

She finished by saying that she didn't want to talk
too long because the youth themselves had to be given
a chance to speak.

Next to her sat a young man in a beret, worn not in
the French style, pulled over one ear, but at the back of
his head like a relaxed chef. He got to his feet as the girl
sat down modestly to applause, and delivered a piece he
seemed to have learnt by heart.

Hurly saw at once that his attention was not on
telling them anything, but on winning the approval of
the girl who had spoken before. He adopted the posture
of a teacher, the voice of a preacher, and spoke words of
bitterness, not only against the police who he said
arrested black people for nothing, but against the people
in the audience who had not done anything about it.
He finished to scant applause and asked for questions.
There were none. The audience had been stunned, and
were partly shy, partly ashamed in case these political
people began to point fingers at them and ask them what
they'd been doing and tell them what they should have
been doing.

Kwate had referred to these politicos as 'Shapesters'.

Hurly tried to give this word some meaning, looking at the people behind the chairman's table and the people standing up around the hall looking as though they were in charge.

'So you're satisfied with the sort of lives that capitalism imposes on you?' the man in the beret said, looking sideways at the girl for approval. She frowned.

'Yeah,' Hurly said and the crowd laughed.

A flicker of uncertainty crossed the speaker's face. He scanned the audience, and then shook his head in exaggerated sorrow. 'The brother over there says "yeah". An American "yeah". You see, some people want to admit it. That's where they will remain, where black people have always been, smoking weed and jumping up in carnival and at the blues and snatching bags and behaving like lumpen elements without consciousness.'

'Oi, don't talk loose, there might be Special Branch!' a voice shouted from the audience. Again there was laughter.

The speaker had lost the audience. He struggled to regain it. 'Some people don't want to see what the white man doing to us. They just like to dress up sharp-sharp and go betting shop and wear all kind of hat and satin shirt...'

'I thief your mother money to buy it?' Hurly said, and found that his voice was louder than he had intended.

'Only time will tell,' the speaker persisted, raising his voice in turn. 'Everything is "real cool" until the blood start flow and fire begin to burn.'

The girl got to her feet and the man sat down. She resumed lecturing the audience. Hurly looked around for Slingo who had spotted a potential customer and had gone to sit next to him. He was speaking to this man who was wearing a fur coat with dark glasses and, abruptly, he got up and went to the door. The man in the fur coat followed him out.

'. . . calling on the youth to give up hustling and be conscious of what sort of reputation they are getting black people . . .' the girl was saying urgently.

Hurly waited for two minutes and when Slingo didn't come back, he got up and followed him out of the hall. Slingo was at the door looking very pleased with himself.

As they walked home, Hurly wondered about whether he should try and be what the girl said he should be. He decided it wasn't possible. 'Good meeting,' he said to Slingo, because he felt guilty for having brought him there, wasted his evening perhaps.

'Yeah, nice, nice, nice,' Slingo agreed, his fist tightening around the wad of pound notes he had acquired from the man with the fur.

Eleven

To Rupert, Edwina pretended that she didn't know Kwate. She never mentioned him, and when he was in the house, he understood that he was to give Rupert no indication that she went to him from time to time. She would disappear for a day or two and come back as though she had never been away. Rupert assumed that she was going to see Michael, that he was failing her by not being able to take her out and spend money on her. He was ashamed of asking her for money, but she gave it to him tactfully and paid for him wherever they went. She bought him clothes; she tried to buy him books.

Edwina allowed him to believe that she was with Michael. She felt that it kept him from treating her as he had told her that his step-father treated his mum. She cleaned and cooked for him, but even though he didn't like it, she would leave food in the kitchen for Slingo when she cooked, not suspecting that Rupert imagined that she had a secret scene with Slingo. He hated it when she went to Slingo's room at night, attracted by the sounds and the promise of a smoke.

She was making a fool of herself and of him, Rupert thought.

Slingo could feel this tension, too, and he amused himself with it. He would say, 'Woman leave you and gone,' when Edwina stayed away. Or he would say, 'Her father must be an MP or something, the way she talk. Why you don't go visit their house and rip them off?'

Rupert couldn't afford to show Slingo that he was jealous. With him he always behaved as though Edwina was somebody he was using as a convenience for the moment. He had to give out that women were no bother to him, they would come and they would go, and he could treat them just as casually as Slingo did.

With Edwina, he let his jealousy loose. If he had to stop what he suspected, he had to stop *her*.

'Do you lend Slingo any money?' he asked her.

'Don't be mad, I'd never get it back,' she said, but Rupert was sure that Slingo was hustling off her.

One Saturday Slingo returned home in the afternoon with a load of stuff he said he'd acquired: a couple of pairs of boots, a new amplifier, a pin-striped three piece suit, a leather coat and stuff like that. When Edwina got home Rupert asked her if she'd pulled any deal with Slingo.

'With whom? What deal?'

'Where's your cheque book and your credit cards?'

'In my bag. I don't know what you're getting at,' she protested and groped in the bottom of her bag. Too deliberately, Rupert thought, she squatted down and emptied the contents of the bag onto the carpet and looked through it. 'I must have left it at Michael's,' she said. 'I thought I had it; I can't understand it.'

A week later Rupert noted to himself that she had a new cheque book but he didn't mention it to her. She must have given it to Slingo to forge cheques.

When he was with Rupert, Slingo would needle him as if to see how far he could push the boy. It was a sadistic game.

'Your wife teach you to make your bed and cook your tea?'

Rupert wouldn't react.

'Is her husband a butty-man?'

Or if Slingo was surrounded by his friends he'd say, 'Rupert keep a nice little thing in the back room there. She have the boy working hard, hard, but the woman tell me she need a man, not a pickney boy.'

One day Slingo brought in a cardboard carton and left it in the hallway downstairs. Rupert checked it and saw that it had several reels of movie film in it. That night, in his room he confronted Edwina.

'Has Slingo asked you to make this film?'

'He asked me months ago, in front of you. I think they've abandoned the whole project.'

'Who's they?'

'Slingo and the people he was going to make it with. You know how scatty they are. I never thought they'd be able to organise it anyway.'

Rupert suspected that she wasn't telling the truth.

'You know what film they want you to make?'

'Some youth thing, isn't it?'

'You don't know what that man's getting you into.'

'Don't start that again. I'm perfectly capable of looking after myself.'

'I doubt it. You think Slingo's a big superstar hustler, but he's just a bag-snatching small time crook.'

'You're beginning to sound like Michael.'

Rupert caught the distinct tone of dishonesty in her voice.

'And you're trying to cover up something, ain't you?'

'Look, let's stop this squabbling. You're getting paranoid.'

'Slingo is a pimp, and you behave in front of everyone here like one of the women he's running.'

'I don't know what you're talking about.'

'You know what I'm talking about, you just come to

this ghetto looking for a bit of black, didn't you, and you don't care who you get it off of.'

'Don't talk filth to me. Anyway, there's not much chance of getting much off you is there?'

Rupert grabbed her by the arm and tried to turn her round to look into his face. She jerked loose of him.

'Don't try that rough stuff on me.'

'You going to make the film with Slingo, aren't you! That's where you were gone yesterday. You think I'm stupid.' Rupert was shouting now.

'All right I am, and you can't stop me. I'm fed up of being pushed around by you. I've also told Slingo that it's no good asking you to co-star in this great film because you can't get it up. Wouldn't make a very hot skin-flick would it.'

Rupert felt a red flash of anger fall across his vision. He doubled his leg and kicked her in the stomach. It was a satisfying blow.

'Don't hit me!' Edwina screamed and Rupert, totally consumed now by confusing rage, struck her with his flat hand across her face. Then he doubled his fist and hit her again. He felt his knuckle connect with the bone of her eye-socket.

'I won't hit you, I'll kill you, you bitch!'

'I'm going, I'm going,' she shouted.

Rupert ran to the kitchen as Edwina dashed out of the room and down the stairs. He caught her on the landing and she saw that he'd grabbed up a kitchen knife. Terror clutched her ribs. She'd never seen him with his face contorted and his eyes blank with anger that made him almost shiver.

He held the knife close to his body and kicked out at her again, catching her in the back as she ran out of the front door.

108

'Tell Slingo he's going to get it, too!' Rupert shouted after her. He heard her footsteps running down the pavement, and turned back into his room in torment.

He had only one thought. He would catch Slingo and confront him. Already Slingo must have made him the laughing stock of the town. Suddenly his suspicion became a certainty. Kwate's remark, Hurly's smirk, Slingo's blatant hints – he should have done something about it before.

There were tears in his eyes as he left the house, but in the cold night air, his rage cooled to calculation. He couldn't let Slingo get away with it. Perhaps all his friends knew that Slingo was 'keeping his breakfast warm for him', as he'd heard Slingo put it when talking about seducing someone's wife or boasting about taking women from other men.

He walked down the 'front line', the row of cafes and liquor shops in which he knew Slingo hung out. He couldn't find him. He walked one way and then the other with some vague idea that he might come across Slingo in the street. Finally he decided to go home, not back to the squat, but to his mother's house.

'You come in here all hours, Rupert! You're after thinking this is a hotel.'

'I got chuck out of my house, Mum. I want to sleep,' he said. He went to his little sister's bedroom and threw himself on the bed.

'You come here in your troubles. I have my troubles, too,' his mum said as she went back to bed. 'Mind, don't wake the girl.'

Rupert couldn't sleep. The idea of Edwina conspiring against him, the image of her and Slingo, kept him awake and restless. Before dawn he got up again and let himself silently out of the door. He walked briskly back to the squat which was at the other end of Brixton. The car was still parked outside. Even though it was four in the morning, Slingo's light was still on.

Rupert opened the door, not certain how he'd react. He still had the knife in the pocket of his jacket. He'd have to say something to Slingo. Maybe he'd allowed his imagination to run riot, and the sight of Slingo would prove that his jealousy had made his reason dizzy, that Edwina would never sink so low as to give herself to this gangling ape of a man.

As he opened the door there was a movement on the upstairs landing. The house always felt damp. The rooms on the bottom floor had plaster peeling off and broken floorboards and smashed window frames. He and Slingo had left them empty, hollow enough to reflect the sound of footsteps in the hall.

'Don't bother come up here,' Slingo's voice said.

Rupert stood still in the light of the half-closed door.

The voice, deep and serious, came round the bend of the staircase. 'Boy, I'm not messing about. You get your arse away from this house, 'cos I got a couple of guns here and I'll shoot you in your big mouth if I see your face in this place.'

Slingo spoke slowly and deliberately. He's trying to scare me, Rupert thought, and his hand tightened round the handle of the kitchen knife. Behind him was the light of the street lamp and ahead of him the darkness to which he was just getting accustomed.

'Is Edwina here?'

'I said to split.'

He hesitated for a moment. 'All right, I'm going,' he

called out, and his voice which he had steeled with defiance, came out as a long whisper. He backed away through the door and slammed it, and walked back to his mother's house.

Twelve

'Rupert's going to kill Slingo, he's gone mad,' Edwina said when Kwate answered the bell.

'I've been up and down these stairs six times this evening. Town going crazy,' Kwate said, letting her into the bulbless hall. He saw that her hair was bushed wildly round her face, that she looked frightened. She'd been running.

'He's serious. Rupert. He went mad on me.'

'The boy beat you?' Kwate grinned. 'He growing up, putting lash on he woman.'

'Don't come that machismo stuff, Kwate, this is serious.'

'Serious for you. Where he beat yuh?'

'That doesn't matter. He's got a knife and he's looking for Slingo. I think he'll do something stupid.'

'You come to sort out the world again. Leave it. Slingo could look after himself.'

'Rupert can't. I think he'll listen to you.'

'What you expect me to do? Go in the night and hold the boy's hand?' Kwate turned and ushered her upstairs. 'If he has a knife, Slingo have a gun,' he said.

'What are you talking about?'

'Slingo is getting a bit desperate now. So why is the punk worked up?'

'About this damn film of Slingo's. He got all prickly and suspicious. Rupert has a lot of problems.' She had

112

learnt the phrase from Kwate. 'He have a lot of problems,' he would say in dismissing anybody.

She didn't like Kwate's amused tolerance of her state of near-panic which she had to fight herself to control. She had told him about how Rupert had behaved in the past few days. When she told him, she had felt it was part of her exploratory adventure. She watched his reaction, which was sympathetic. He had spoken to her about Rupert and Hurly and how they were the great black hope of the future.

'Except white women, they always mess up the youth's head. I've seen too much fight over white pussy in this town.'

She hated him when he put on this arrogant mood and tone. She felt with all of them, except Rupert perhaps, that they lived on the edge of an unspoken violence. Kwate was capable of doing anything, even though he never seemed to lose his temper.

Kwate had given her no indication downstairs in the hallway, or while climbing the long flight of stairs that they'd find Slingo sitting in his room. He greeted her with an obscene grin as she walked through.

'Boy lost his cool and put a beating on Ed here,' Kwate said.

'So you ain't going home now. No place to go, judgement and mercy gone,' Kwate said as Edwina settled into the only chair in the room.

'He might come up here,' Edwina said.

'Don't worry about him, I'll deal with him.'

'We were going to start shooting tomorrow,' Slingo said. 'You've gone and screw it up now.'

'I never said I'd do your bloody film. What do you think I am?'

'You asking me your price? I ain't your ponce,' Slingo said.

Edwina looked at Kwate and he took the hint in her expression. She couldn't take Slingo's nonsense tonight. 'Leave it for tonight,' he said authoritatively to Slingo.

Slingo rose slowly from the bed and put his leather coat on. 'You keep the machinery,' he said to Kwate, and, 'All right, I'll check you up my house,' to Edwina. Kwate went onto the landing and walked part of the way down the stairs with him.

'You backed out of the film too?' Kwate asked, coming back into the room and putting some music on the player.

'Kwate, you know very well I never consented to do anything of the sort.'

'What's the difference between one thing and another? If you're a go-go dancer, you could be a stripper. There was good breads in it.'

She knew what he was alluding to. 'I thought that was something personal between you and me.'

'There's no personal thing with me and anybody.'

There was a sinking feeling in Edwina's stomach. The ghost of a suspicion she had had as she ran to Kwate's place, had taken full body.

'What have you done with those snaps?'

'What snaps?'

'The ones I let you take of me. I want the whole reel.'

'It's still in the camera.'

'Where is it?'

She felt foolish, looking at the deliberate remoteness, the distance in his face. Kwate sat on the edge of the bed with a little mirror in his hand, his tongue stretching the skin on his cheek as though he were examining his face for pimples. 'Skin dry up in your climate,' he said.

'You've given them to Slingo, haven't you?'

'Your photo ain't worth nothing. Slingo took the reel to develop it. There's plenty girls will pose for anybody. You can't sell them pictures, nobody want to buy them. So relax, nobody's hustling you.'

'Maybe Rupert found the photographs in Slingo's room or something.'

'I'm a photographer. I could take what picture I like. What it got to do with the boy?'

'You want to explain that to him?'

'They're not developed yet, anyway. I just gave them to him today. You want them back, you can have them back. I don't want to sell pin-ups of your ugly white body anyway.'

She hadn't seen Kwate like this before. She knew that when he was annoyed he used the word 'white' to sting and insult her, but she had always taken this as a game, a battle of wits that was a test of her self-assurance. Edwina pressed the small of her back where Rupert had kicked her. She told herself that she didn't care if Kwate was contemptuous, he couldn't rule her with his contempt. He pushed around the black boys who hero-worshipped him, but he treated even them with more respect. She should never have consented to allowing him to take photographs of her. Kwate had set up two spot lamps and a camera on a tripod and had said to her he wanted to take pictures of her. It had flattered her, even though he asked her in a totally business-like tone. He had induced her to take bits of clothing off, and after an evening of making love, he had sat her on a stool in the nude and snapped her relaxed body and sullen but spirited expression.

Perhaps she was being paranoid about the pictures, she thought. Maybe he *had* given them to Slingo just to develop and add to the folders he had in the corner of his room. Rupert didn't know anything; he couldn't. There was nothing much to know in any case. It wasn't his business. She had the right to do as she pleased; she wasn't going to step out of one relationship and move into another repressed 'scene', as they called it. A sense of failure struck her.

'You really treat me like white trash, don't you? I don't mean a thing to you, your hustles and your ego are all that ever matter to you.'

'You used the word,' Kwate replied. 'Far as I know there are only two kinds of white people; those who afraid of blacks and those who aren't. You white girls who hang around Brixton is scared of we. You come looking to put a little collar round Rupert's neck. It's him need protection from you, not you from him. In the end you'll go back to your butty-man husband who'll become headmaster and lick little boys with a stick. You like to eat good and live good and drive your car, and you want a bit of black under your control because it something that frightens your mind.'

'That's a lot of shit. Racist shit. I treated Rupert like a friend.'

'That's why you come sleep with me and hide it from him?'

'He wouldn't understand. I have my own needs, too. He's just a boy.'

'He's your boy, but I'm not your man.'

'You better get that film back.'

'Or you'll call your husband and ask him to beat me?' Kwate laughed.

'All right, play it that way,' Edwina said, rising from the bed, her hands in her pockets. 'Be seeing you.'

He is a vulture, she thought as she walked out into the

night. He lives off the dead feelings of those around him. Maybe he was right, though. She had had enough of Rupert and of Kwate, too. Yes, she had been afraid of something, a quality of ambition it was, that threatened to burst out from them. She remembered thinking they were men in a hurry with nowhere to go, and she began to wonder now, listening to her own footsteps on the deserted street, where it was she was going.

Thirteen

Edwina groped in her pocket for a twopenny piece. She'd left all her stuff at Rupert's. There was some change in her denim pockets, but no tuppence. It took ages for the operator to pick up the call. She wanted a reverse charge call. She gave the number and waited tensely for Michael to pick up the receiver. He would know it was her.

His voice was sleepy. 'It's rather late isn't it?'

'Michael, I want to come over.'

'This is all very sudden,' he said, sarcastically.

'I'll explain when I get there, all right?'

'What's wrong, no room at the bordello tonight?'

'Please, Michael, I have a right to the place, you know that. I just want to come and sleep. I'd like to talk to you too, of course, but you don't sound as though you want to talk to me. I'm sorry about this evening, about some other things too.'

'We won't argue your rights over the phone. I'll leave the door on the latch.'

'Michael, I haven't got any money. I'll hop a cab, will you lend me some?'

'What happened to the car?'

She hesitated. 'It broke down, I've left it in a side street.'

'Where?'

'Look, I'll talk when I get there, right?' She could tell from his last questions that though he was annoyed, he'd be awake to pay for the cab. He wanted her to return.

She hadn't seen him for weeks. He hadn't tried to contact her at school. In the cab it struck her that he might have another woman there. She'd have to be very careful.

'You've just dropped in for a visit, have you?' Michael said pretending to be more annoyed than he really was. When he put the phone down, he'd gone and brushed his hair and gargled with toothpaste to get rid of the stink of stale sleep.

'Can I make coffee?'

'Do as you like. You have rights to the place, exercise them.'

'I didn't mean that in a bullying way.'

He was looking at her eye. He could see that she'd been hit, but he suppressed his instinct to ask her how it had happened. He could see she was uncertain, and while it made him feel slightly triumphant to have her sitting in the kitchen at one in the morning, he also felt sorry for her. She had suffered some defeat. If he wanted, he could make her earn her passage back to him. That's what he'd been longing for, that was how he saw her little adventure with Rupert ending, and it gave him some satisfaction to see his prediction taking shape.

'You haven't been in an accident, have you?'

'No, nothing like that.'

'Trouble with the boys, huh?'

'Oh, please don't be frivolous, I'll explain in the morning. I need some time to think.'

'The bed in my study's still there. I'll go and sleep there. You can sleep in my bed.'

She noticed that he called it 'his' bed. 'So it's "my" bed now?'

'Has been for some time, Edwina.' She caught a low note of regret in his sentence.

'I'd like to sleep in our room, there's no need for you to move into the study.'

'We should let the cosiness take its own shape instead of forcing it, don't you think?'

'I don't want to force anything, I just didn't mean to put you out. It's my fault that things haven't worked out recently, for you and me, and for a long time I suppose. I didn't want to walk in and take over.'

'Not much chance of that. I have my rights too.'

'Sure.'

As he pretended to be asleep beside her, Edwina lay awake and her mind turned over vivid images of Rupert's angry face. What would she tell Michael? She wanted to tell him the truth but she constantly told herself that the truth wasn't merely the facts. It was her excuse for not being truthful about facts. The bed felt warm, and as she looked at Michael's naked back, getting slightly fatty, Kwate's insult about her 'ugly white body' came back to her.

Fourteen

Rupert got off the tube at Victoria, waited patiently in the queue at the top of the escalator, and then with a quick dash, overtook it and ran past the ticket collector and up the stairs into the street.

'Bastard,' the ticket collector shouted at him, his tone admitting that Rupert had got away, that he couldn't be bothered to chase him.

Rupert was still nervous of pulling this stunt, but he had no option. His mother, who had accepted his return reluctantly, wouldn't give him a penny. 'Go look for work,' she had said to him on his second day of lounging around the flat. He didn't even have a spare change of clothes with him. On the third day he went to Kwate's and told him that he'd decided to leave the place he shared with Slingo, omitting to mention why. He talked about Nick, the boy he used to work the Portobello with. Kwate listened. Rupert had been hoping to find Hurly there, so that he could ask Hurly to fetch his things from the house. He had to ask Kwate to go with him. Slingo wasn't there. Edwina's car had been moved. Rupert made a quick dash upstairs and picked up as much as he could, stuffing it into paper bags.

At the corner of Victoria Street, Rupert pulled out Nick's neatly written-up diary. He had told his mother he was going to find himself a job, but had gone out to Nick's place. Under the heading VICTORIA, Nick had written in ten addresses. Next to the address, written in a different pen, were ten names, randomly invented. Nick had told him that there was absolutely nothing to worry about. All he had to do was get an *A to Z*, go to those addresses during office hours when the front doors to the hallways would be open, and if there was no one about, pick up the parcels with those names on them and bring them to him. He said he'd give him fifty pounds for every district he covered. He'd been to Jermyn Street in the West End the day before and it had been easy enough. In two of the buildings he met hall porters on the stairs, and then he just went up the lift, waited a few minutes on one of the landings and came down again, marking the address with a cross for Nick to return to.

He knew that the parcels could have almost anything, from electric typewriters to chest-expanding machines, fancy barometers, clothes, hundreds of other things. Nick had perfected a new deal, he told Rupert. He went down to a place in Fleet Street on a certain day of the week when they sold off large bundles of old papers with mail-order coupons in them. He simply filled these out in different names and addresses of flats and offices with open front doors to which parcels would be delivered. He or Rupert could pick up the goods and flog them.

If the parcels got too heavy, he could take a taxi, Nick told him. He would pay. Rupert tried to look decent on this job. He had cleaned up and wore a shirt and one of his step-father's ties.

He hadn't told Kwate or Hurly the details of the racket. He knew they were desperate for a bit of easy money, but the closer he kept Nick's business to himself, the more unlikely it was that other hustlers would muscle in on it.

Rupert came to the first address. There were name

plates on the door. They announced the occupancy of six different firms. To the left of the hallway there were lockers for the post, no enquiry window, no hall porter, nothing. On top of the lockers fifty letters were scattered, along with three parcels.

Harold Jay. Yes!

He picked it up and walked out. Easy as telling margarine from butter.

As he was walking out, a man passed him in the hall-way. 'Which floor for Dempster's?'

'I think the top. I'm just passing messages.'

The man moved on. 'Should have picked a nicer day.'

It was a long, light parcel, and looked as though it could have been a pair of skis in it.

The next address. A yellow door, again with office name plates on it. A much larger, modernised hallway with the mail laid out on a table at the bottom of the stairs. Another parcel. He read the name on it. He smiled when he recognised the name as that of a boy who had been in school with him and Nick, a tall gang-ling boy who was called Timothy Satchell, though all the kids called him 'Timmy Handbag', because he had a certain reputation.

The parcel was fairly large. He piled it on the other and walked out. He put the diary in his pocket and began to peel the label off the parcel in the street. He would pick up one more, and then, depending on whether it was light or heavy, he would call a taxi or move on to the next one and try to finish the district that afternoon.

He walked down the street, balancing the parcels. A white car, parked on the opposite side, started and drove up alongside him. A man leapt out of the driver's seat and another came out from the far side.

'Come here, you.'

Rupert turned at the sound of the voice and froze. He thought his best ploy would be to pretend they weren't talking to him and he began to walk faster. The man dressed in a dark tweed jacket ran up to him and caught him by the shoulder.

'I said come here!'

'I'm waiting for a taxi,' Rupert stammered.

'Let's look at that shopping,' the man said producing a card from his pocket with the cinematic gesture of a detective inspector.

Fifteen

Rupert phoned Michael to sign his bail papers. As he had expected, Michael turned up. The police refused to let Rupert go until they got a lead on Nick, but Rupert held out. He told them that he had picked up a few parcels the week before but that he had disposed of the goods in Portobello market, a few things, not very much. The police brought a pile of three hundred written out mail-order coupons and threw it on the table in the interrogation room. 'You'll go down for ten years on this lot,' the detective said. 'If you help us and give the names of the real people behind this racket, we'll let you off.'

Rupert said he wanted to see a lawyer.

'You ain't got a lawyer, Sunshine,' the detective replied, 'and you won't be having mummy's dumplings for dinner tonight if you don't tell us who you flog the stuff to.'

Rupert phoned Michael's school from the court the next day. The magistrate agreed to let him out on bail after Michael said he'd known Rupert for six years. He agreed, as Rupert had known he would, to stand as his surety.

'Thanks, man,' was all Rupert said to him.

'I've got to get back to school,' Michael said. He had not mentioned the matter to Edwina.

'We are to bring three hundred more charges,' the police said to the magistrate who leaned over and looked as though his specs were going to fall off.

'*How* many?'

Rupert went home and that evening he went to Kwate's. For a few hours they talked about how the police had treated him and what he could do to get himself a lawyer who would get him off the charge.

'They going to send you down, boy,' Kwate said. 'You're going to get some heavy pieces for this job. You should have told them you was working for the white man and fingered him.'

Rupert disagreed. Nick had given him money in the past when he was broke.

'You'll need some money to get out of the country. Go to the Caribbean for a few years and if you come back they'll have forgotten that you was on a charge.'

'What about the bail?'

'Not your problem, is it?'

The idea of leaving the country had taken root in Rupert's head. He attached a fantasy to it. If he could get the money together, he would take Edwina with him. He wouldn't go to the Caribbean, he would go to the States or to Canada where he could get a flat with her. She had murdered his ego, but she could bring it back to life again. He'd forgive her.

The robbery of the mini-cab firm was Kwate's idea, or so it seemed to Rupert. Kwate proposed it to him and to Hurly with the air of a general who had hand-picked the volunteers for a special operation.

'We could make two pieces, two thousand pounds each,' he said. Neither Rupert nor Hurly doubted that there'd be that much money in the mini-cab firm.

Kwate said only enough to arouse Rupert's curiosity. He couldn't understand why Kwate didn't do it alone, if it was so easy, but he didn't want to ask. Kwate would speak generally about the way in which black people couldn't keep secrets and couldn't work together, but sometime somewhere they were going to have to.

Kwate outlined the plan to him and Hurly one night in his room and said they could do it if they wanted next week.

Neither Kwate nor Hurly had told Rupert that Slingo would be involved, that he was going to be their driver. Rupert didn't even know exactly where they were going. He was afraid to ask lest his curiosity be mistaken for nervousness. Kwate asked them to meet him outside a particular club on the Friday evening. Rupert turned up separately from Hurly and they both waited on the pavement for almost an hour and then walked round the block to see if there were other entrances to that particular club.

An hour later, Kwate drove up in a Ford Cortina with Slingo wearing a hat low over his forehead. Slingo was driving, slouched in the driver's seat.

'I ain't going with him,' Rupert said.

Kwate came out onto the pavement. 'Come on, boy, business is business. Don't mix your woman trouble with your work.'

He gripped Rupert's shoulder. 'If you terrorised now, you could go home.'

Rupert climbed in the back of the car and Hurly went round to the outside.

'Why are we going by car?'

'You want to hop a bus after?'

Slingo turned into Oxford Street and again down Regent Street, heading for the lower side of Soho. In one of the side streets he parked the car, and leaving the three of them sitting there, he went down some steps into a basement and re-emerged with two guitar cases. Hurly opened the back door and took them from him. Rupert felt that he had been left out of all this pre-arrangement because Slingo was involved. For some reason, Kwate wanted him on this job and had been very careful what he said to him about Slingo.

'Sweet, sweet music,' Slingo said. 'Sweet soul music. Rebel music, taking over.'

They drove off.

'We're two hours late,' Rupert said. 'Is it still all right?'

'Later the better,' Hurly said, when the other two didn't answer.

'Open the case and take one each,' Kwate said to Hurly.

Hurly opened the cases at his feet. Kwate leaned across the front seat, picked up a revolver and held it out, below the level of the car windows, to Rupert.

'What for?'

'It's not loaded, just to scare someone if we meet them,' Kwate replied.

He passed the revolver to Hurly who slipped it into the pocket of his denim jacket.

Rupert was thinking that Slingo didn't have a licence to drive a car. 'You don't have licence, do you? Suppose we get picked up on a check with all this stuff here?'

'Shut up, boy, lysuns never improved people driving. More people killed by people with lysuns than without.'

Rupert felt Slingo had been drinking. It gave him some comfort to feel that the hard hustler had to strengthen himself for this ride. 'Too many people involved,' he said.

'Look, you want to get out?' Kwate asked turning round in his seat. Kwate was on edge.

'He must tell he girl-friend. How is she?' Slingo said.

Kwate put his arm out and gripped Rupert by the knee. He looked almost pleadingly at Rupert to avoid replying to Slingo. It was the first time, Rupert thought, that he had shown that there was some understanding between them. He had felt that to Kwate it didn't matter if you remained a stranger because he wasn't interested in what he could do for you or you for him. The job was a partnership, pure in its definition of self-interests.

'Give me one,' Rupert said to Hurly. 'You sure it's not loaded. I mean I don't want to fool around with that thing.'

Hurly handed Rupert a pistol from the floor of the car. Rupert worked his backside off the seat and with a quick crouching motion hefted the gun and thrust it inside his pocket. It stuck out. He pulled it out and put it down the front of his shirt, tucking it into his trousers.

'You take an iron, boy,' Slingo teased. 'Those irons good for holding off lickle boys who come after men with a knife.'

'Stop your fockries,' Kwate snapped at Slingo, and turning to Rupert, 'It's all right, he's terrified out of his mind. Man's had too much Special Brew.'

T.S.O.B.—E

129

Sixteen

Kwate switches the television on. For two days he has forbidden anyone to turn the knob, and he pulls the plug out of the socket and sleeps with the lead under his body when it is his turn to rest, to make sure that the others don't turn on the news. He wears the gun over his shoulder now, with the white man's discarded shirt tied in a sash to its barrel and trigger-guard. Kwate has been thinking hard. He is morose, but apart fom the ban on TV, he allows the others to relax.

The police have sent up the ingredients of a recipe which Hurly sent down to them. He says he wants to do some cooking and, after a day, two saucepans arrive with a plastic laundry basket containing vegetables and groceries. Hurly has already cooked them one meal and now the girl is in the kitchen cooking another with him. Rupert plays cards with the white man, and the boy sulks all day, behaving sullenly with them all. The only person who can get through to him is the girl, and she coaxes him to eat the fried plantains that Hurly has cooked. He refuses at first, but hunger gets the better of him.

'This flour no good,' says Hurly, 'and they didn't send suet for dumplings. Tcha.'

'Make an Irish stew instead,' the girl says.

The kitchen now smells lived-in, with the stink of spices. The girl helps Hurly with the dishes and they chat pleasantly, like colleagues at a dirty job rather than captor and hostage. Kwate makes the white man tidy up, and he does it without a word but with daggers of unspoken resentment in his eyes. The man is sure that he is going to come out of here alive, Rupert thinks. He is the kind of white man who pretends he knows how to repair aeroplanes and would have a damn good try if they'd hijacked him in a plane and something had gone wrong with the controls.

'I just eat and I hungry again,' Hurly says to the girl.

'You didn't sleep much.'

'I couldn't.'

She looks up from where she's slicing onions and catches Hurly's eye for a moment. He averts his eyes. She keeps looking at me as though I could let her go if I want, he thinks. It makes him uncomfortable. Yet today in her gaze there is also the recognition of something else. It is as though she's telling herself that this one is just an ordinary boy, no gangster, no monster.

'I get hungry dreams,' he says.

'You mean greedy dreams.'

'You are a man-watcher,' he comments.

He feels easy with her when he isn't under the eyes of the others. He wears the Smith and Wesson tucked into his trousers. He has been to the lavatory and pulled the bullet out of the chamber and put it into the flush tank. He is wearing a dummy gun because he says to himself that he doesn't want it blowing up in his trousers while he's asleep, and he doesn't want Kwate to know that he's unloaded it.

On the TV screen, Big Ben strikes.

'Oi, in here,' Rupert shouts to Hurly, who grabs the butt of his revolver and dashes to the kitchen door, his head turning quickly to make sure of the girl. Hurly behaves like a man on drugs, making sudden movements. He is letting the girl know that he is determined not to be thought of as harmless. At a pinch, he would kill to survive.

'The bells of Babylon,' Rupert says, turning his head to see if Kwate has caught the remark.

The siege is the first headline.

Newsreader: In London the mini-cab siege enters its seventh day. We bring you, in Part One, a remarkable piece of film, shot as the news came through of the siege's first victim. Police have formally charged the fourth member of the ransom gang. Derek Obute interviews the mother of one of the gunmen of Corbett Street. In Libya, President Gaddafi has accused the United States of....

(Scene: Outside the siege. Shot of police cars and the entrance to 37 Corbett Street.)

Newsreader: Senior police officers today admitted that they can make no prediction about the outcome of the Corbett Street siege. Earlier today, they confirmed reports that the fourth man in the siege, the man who is said to have driven the getaway car, has turned state's witness and will testify against the gunmen in the siege when they are brought to trial. From the press release of his testimony, it seems that the siege was not part of a robbery plan that went wrong. Notes have been exchanged between the police and the gunmen who still refuse to release the twelve-year-old son of Mr Photopoulos who died in hospital yesterday after being released as a hostage from Corbett Street. In another part of the city, police have cordoned off the house of Hurlington Macaulay, one of the gunmen.

(Scene: Street corner in Brixton. Derek Obute stands, microphone in hand.)

Derek Obute: Here in this street in Brixton, people have gathered outside the home of one of the gunmen of the mini-cab siege. Police have cordoned off the street after violent incidents involving the mother and step-father of the gunman known as 'Hurly'. We spoke with Mrs Violet Macaulay, Hurly's mother, earlier this morning.

(Scene: The interior of the Macaulay home. Mrs Macaulay sits on a chair before a tiled mantelpiece. Family photographs are ranged behind her.)

Derek Obute: Mrs Macaulay, you told the police earlier that you were making an appeal to your son and to all the gunmen, boys with whom you are acquainted, to give themselves up.

Mrs Macaulay: Yes, that is what I have said. They must realise what it is his mother having to live with daily here. I said that the police must let my son go because I pray like a mother for the speedy return of my son.

Derek Obute: Well, yes. You know that the men who are holding the hostages have been given a television set. Do you hope your son is watching this programme and have you –

Mrs Macaulay: Well, he had better hear his mother, and I hope so. And I been to the Jamaican embassy and to other people, friends of ours who helping with this problem, you know, and they say the police lie about that embassy because they tell me personally that they have not banned my son.

Derek Obute (a bit flustered): The embassy did make a statement in the early days of the siege, saying they would not accept the . . . er . . . the gunmen.

Mrs Macaulay: My Hurly is a good boy. My boy is not

a boy of violence unless he pushed into it and the police they –

Derek Obute: You have actually applied to the police for protection. Obviously you feel that there is strong feeling –

Mrs Macauley: Yes, I feel very strong about it, Mr Derek, because a lot of reporters and television people and everyone been coming daily to my house and I fed up of answering their stupid question. What do they want a mother to say when they call she son all sort of name? Eh?

Derek Obute: Thank you very much, Mrs Macaulay. This is Derek Obute, reporting from Brixton.

Newsreader: Yesterday the siege claimed its fifth victim indirectly when we learned that Mr Photopoulos, father of twelve-year-old Panos still being held by the gunmen, had died in hospital. News that he had had another stroke came when our interviewer, Tony Green, was with the family of Mr Photopoulos. Mrs Photopoulos, mother of Panos, was making an appeal to the gunmen to release her son.

(Interviewer sits before a large Greek lady leaning forward in an armchair. Behind her, standing at the edge of the chair is her eldest son who keeps a hand on her shoulder throughout the interview.)

Mrs Photopoulos: Of course we hope for his release. Your heart cannot be in two place. I am relief and I am worry also, both same time. My son never harm nobody. He go to school with a lot of coloured people. My husband always work with coloured people. Why should men do this to my poor family?

(Her eyes are swollen with crying; she lifts a handkerchief to them. She is about to go on when a girl dashes onto the screen. Viewers can see only her back and she

shouts in Greek to her mother. Mrs Photopoulos gets up from the chair and holding her palms out, gives a cry. Her son rushes to support her. The voice of the interviewer announces that Mr Photopoulos has just suffered another stroke in hospital. End of film clip.)

Newsreader: With that tragic news we end Part One of the News. We will bring you, in Part Two, film of a speech which President. . . .

Kwate rises and switches the set off.

The boy, on his knees now in front of the TV set, is aware that all eyes are on him. His mouth twitches and he lets out a sniff. The hot tears begin to roll down his cheeks.

'Ai,' Kwate says to him, 'that not for you, that for us. Your father ain't dead. Nobody dead. The police playing games with us. They lie about Slingo, and they lie about having names. They want to terrorise us and demoralise us.'

The rest are aware that Kwate is talking to them, not to the boy.

'I want to go home. Let me go home,' the boy wails.

'You bloody well killed him, didn't you,' the white man now says, staring at Kwate.

'Just everybody keep cool,' Kwate says and his arm goes uncertainly to the shotgun.

'We have to let the boy go,' Hurly says, answering the appeal which he sees in the girl's eyes and watching the boy sobbing now and looking up at him.

'What's the matter with you? You giving orders here?' Kwate demands.

'We've got to do something,' Rupert says lamely. 'They can have us now for . . .' He hesitates to say the word.

'They can have you. They ain't having me and they ain't having the boy. You see what Hurly's mother say? The police haven't been to no embassy. They give us this thing here to freak us out. And the raas clot cooking.' Now there's an edge of confidence, menace, even accusation in Kwate's voice and the other two acknowledge its authority. 'Psychology!' he barks, looking at Hurly.

'This thing needs discussion. We ought to ask the police to see some people, someone we can trust.' Rupert is only half-convinced by Kwate's argument.

Kwate feels he is losing the initiative. There is a nasty look on the white man's face, as though he would leap at them, force them to shoot him. Kwate goes to the window and shouts to Burgess.

'Oi, we want to talk to you.'

There's no reply. He tries again and then again. It is as though there are no listeners among the police or the crowd outside. The silence, almost total outside, is puzzling. Kwate doesn't pull the curtains back as he usually does.

Each one of them is thinking that if the police have moved the crowd, cordoned off the place perhaps, they are getting ready to make some serious move, perhaps to rush them.

'Games, games, games,' Kwate says.

Seventeen

The early morning light hits Rupert's eyelids, and its soft heat coaxes them open. It is strange, because in that room they have been used to waking in shadow. In his dream he has seen Hurly's mother and confused her with his own. Her voice calls him from somewhere outside a darkened room, and his mind struggles awake from this hypnotic call as though he is swimming out of some dark depths of water, his lungs bottled and bursting for the surface.

He sits up and the blanket falls away from his shoulder. He looks around the room. Kwate is asleep when he should be sitting on the stool by the door. He is curled up beside the stool and looks fierce in his sleep, even though his arms are tucked between his drawn-up knees like those of a sleeping baby. The white man is snoring. The girl sleeps beside him. Only Hurly is awake.

The strange light in the room makes it seem smaller than it usually appears. Hurly is sitting by the open window. He has obviously moved the table that was supposed to block off the window and has drawn the curtains fully back.

'Hey! What's happening?' Rupert whispers.

His impulse is to grab Hurly and pull him down. He's cracked under the strain, Rupert thinks, seeing his mum on telly and realising that there's no way out of this place. Hurly sits impassive. He is wearing Kwate's tam on his head and leaning on the window sill.

Rupert remembers that Kwate tied up the young boy the night before and left him in the kitchen on some blankets. They couldn't stop the boy sobbing and Kwate said he didn't like to do it, but it had to be done. The others didn't stop him.

Now Hurly turns his head slowly. His eyes look distant, but they call Rupert to the window.

'They ain't going to shoot us. There's no one there,' he says.

Rupert goes up to the window and looks out. The street below is completely deserted. It looks as though it has been washed. The police barriers are still there, but there isn't a person in sight. The windows on the houses opposite are curtained and blank. It's like looking at a picture, the silence of it.

'Somethin's goin' on. Police pull out,' Rupert says and looks questioningly at Hurly. Should they wake Kwate? he is thinking. He pushes his nose right up against the window but can't see beyond the ledge if there are policemen or anyone else in the doorway or along the wall of their own building.

'The Trojan thing,' Hurly says. 'You know that story.'

It strikes Rupert that Hurly has gone mad and he looks carefully at his face.

'Beware the Greeks bearing gifts,' Hurly says slowly, recollecting.

'Are you all right?'

'I hear this story in school, boy. The Greek army leave the shores and them Trojans wake up one morning and find all the ships and soldiers gone, and on the beach they leave a wooden horse.'

'There's no horse,' Rupert says. He's heard the story, too. 'Look, close the curtains, there might be spiders. They're up to some tricks.'

'They want to tempt us to come out and then light-ning strike and the valiant shall taste of death.'

'Just draw the curtains,' Rupert says and pulls at Hurly's shoulder. He draws Hurly into the room and drapes the curtains back into place.

Kwate begins to stir. He sits bolt upright.

'It's all right, they're asleep,' Rupert says to him, and goes to the kitchen. The boy is also asleep, breathing deeply, rhythmically.

'The street empty, the police gone,' he tells Kwate.

'Gone nowhere,' Kwate says, rubbing his eyes. He goes into the kitchen and washes his face.

The hostages wake up, hearing the bustle in the room. It is very mysterious, Rupert thinks. They don't make coffee or get themselves anything to eat. A mood of immobility and hopelessness seems to have settled on all of them.

'Without the help of the community, we going to be stuck here till your hair turn white,' Kwate says.

There have been black people watching in the street throughout the siege. I know West Indians, Rupert thinks: they'll talk endlessly about the siege, but they'll do nothing. In a few days the novelty, the gossip value will wear out.

He wishes they could start all over again. Not the robbery, not this business of the hostages. These people are no good as hostages. Maybe the police think that their lives aren't precious enough to trade for other lives. They should have taken them into the street instead of rushing up the stairs into this trap, taken them at gunpoint in a cab straight to the airport. They may have stood a chance then. Or they could have threatened and released them, and maybe even got away with the money once they were a few miles from the site of the robbery. How would the police know who pulled the job? There are thousands of young blacks and to these people we all look alike anyway. Like the Chinese and Japanese look alike to me, Rupert thinks.

For the first few days he felt as though the world was looking on. Now this room is stale with the smell of the people in it. He wants to get away from them. But how? And where to go? They'd have to find a place in which the laws of life and of people having to pull guns and hustles on other people don't operate. There's no such place. There's no place where you can start life each day as though the last hasn't happened. People just aren't willing to give you that chance.

He thinks of Edwina constantly now. If he ever gets out of this, he'll give her a chance, and she'll give him another short lease on her life.

At about eleven in the morning, after the noise of traffic begins to pervade the room again, the occupants of the siege hear a tramp of feet in the street outside. Hurly doesn't move from where he is sitting on the settee, but Rupert jumps up and looks out from behind the edge of the curtain.

'A demo coming down the road,' he says.

There must be fifty people. They are carrying placards.

'Black people wake up,' Kwate says with a flicker of triumph in his eyes.

'They're white people.'

Kwate rushes to the window. The police are back. They are all over the street, more than he has ever seen before. In front, at the edge of the barrier, stands the line of demonstrators, and behind them a looser crowd, all scrambling for a look.

The demonstrators are chanting something, but Rupert can't make out what it is.

'What the placards say?' Kwate asks.

Rupert reads them aloud: 'KILL THE MURDERERS. END THE SIEGE. POLICE ACTION NOW.'

'The pigs brought them here,' Kwate snaps. 'We could stop them.'

He runs the heel of his hand over the butt of the shot gun and lifts it as though to aim through the window. The chanting breaks into confused shouts.

Kwate puts the shotgun down. The girl comes to the window and looks out.

'The police should send them away,' she says.

'Are they Greeks?' the white man asks her.

The girl doesn't reply. She is watching the effect that the shouting is having on Kwate. He rushes to the kitchen and looks in to see what the boy is doing. He slams the kitchen door.

'The police bring them people here,' he shouts. 'Burgess too damn smart. Burgess is a master, he pull a whole demo on us. Psychology, boy, psychology is a devil.'

Eighteen

Seven days after the siege began the police called on Edwina: two men in plain clothes. She had been dreading their visit, had known it would come.

On the third day she had driven down into the West End and stood amongst the crowd outside. She wanted to forget it all, forget Rupert, put Kwate into the closet in her mind reserved for the things she had bought by mistake, things which wouldn't fit outside the seductive atmosphere of fashion and vanity in a boutique. She couldn't escape the feeling that she had something to do with Rupert being where he was; she had been irresponsible, pushed him to edge of desperation. She hadn't wanted to taunt him. She was surprised, though it had flattered her, that he had taken her offer of intimacy as a promise of something lasting. He had begged for all the strength she could give him and hadn't been able to see her as what she was. Kwate was different. She had never mentioned Kwate to Michael. He was the sort of man that made you feel that anyone was entitled to do anything to anyone else. She could understand how he'd hold hostages. She feared that he'd shoot them too. If Kwate was besieged, he had chosen to be. Rupert – she had been accused by Michael of using Rupert to alleviate her failing sense of herself.

'There's no reason why we can't still be friends,' she had said to Michael. She wanted Rupert to trust her again. It would have been possible. She imagined meeting

Rupert with a black girl pushing a pram some day down the streets of Stockwell or Brixton; she'd stop and be introduced. But now this period of coming to terms with herself was transformed into a wound she would carry with her. The words of a song that Slingo used to play came back to her, and his rhythm beat in her head : *The tables gwyne turn and the fire gwyne burn.*

Michael had so many good phrases, 'If I don't give you a promise of growth,' he said, 'you can't live your tomorrows through me.' He had wanted to talk about what exactly she meant by 'love'. She had wanted to put these abstracts away. She felt she had been taught – no, that she had paid the price of – a lesson.

Edwina first heard of the siege on her radio as she was brushing her hair for school. Michael didn't seem to pay it any attention. The news bulletin didn't give the names of any of those involved. Three men had held up a mini-cab firm; they were holding hostages.

In the staff room, the other teachers were talking about it. All blacks, they said; it was getting serious. Some of the pupils in her fifth year group came up to her in the corridor. She was the one to discuss these things with. They said she knew the boy who done it, didn't she?

Edwina left work early. She drove the car to the squat. There was nobody there. She had a sinking feeling in her stomach. The evening papers were full of it. She went home, waited a couple of hours and drove back. There was no one home. There was no other answer. Slingo didn't work, Rupert wouldn't have found himself a job yet. She went home.

Michael knew what the matter was as soon as he walked in that evening. 'So your lover turned out to be more than a petty mugger. I suppose you think he's a great political hero. Did you help them plan this piece of black consciousness?'

'Michael, stop it. I haven't seen Rupert for.... I swear I haven't seen him. I don't know why....'

'People are difficult, aren't they? They do all sorts of things.'

'You're so bloody smug.'

She stopped him as he was putting his clothes into a case in the bedroom. 'Michael, don't be silly. What are you trying to do? Punish me for your hang-ups?'

'I'm not being silly,' he replied, 'I just want to leave you with your deep and honest concerns for the great black hope. Don't you want to think it over?'

'I have, Michael,' she said. 'I have!'

The inspectors came and sat in the kitchen.

'You know what we want, Mrs Cross,' they announced. 'You are acquainted with Rupert Dowling, and, we have reason to believe, with Aloysius Brown as well.'

'Do you mind if I sit in on this?' Michael enquired.

'We'll require your co-operation, Mr Cross,' said the detective inspector, and to Edwina, 'You're not denying that you know these characters?'

Edwina shook her head.

'Very good. Our Chief Superintendent, you must have heard over the news, he's running this operation, he'd like a word with you.'

'What about?'

'I want to make clear to you and to your husband that this is a kind of social call. We want to make a request. There are no charges against you or anything like that. We want you to help the police.'

'I've got nothing to do with it.'

'No. Not directly of course; we don't believe you have. But we have reason to believe that you have some influence over the lads, over this boy Rupert. Your husband stood bail for him, didn't you? He was your student or something.'

Edwina was frightened. Half-formed questions flashed through her mind.

'There are lives at stake, Mrs Cross, and we believe you can be very helpful.'

'How?'

'We'd like you to come down to the station now and Mr Burgess will explain.'

Chief Superintendent Burgess was very polite. He sent for cups of coffee and sat Edwina down.

'Now please don't misunderstand. I've asked for your help because lives are obviously involved here. . . .'

He began to talk about the drama club and about blacks in South London and how one of their chief concerns was community relations. 'And I'd like to assure you that your name and your husband's name will be left out of this affair entirely. We are looking for a peaceful end to the siege.'

Burgess was sitting across the table from Edwina. He twiddled his thumbs, and looked steadily and seriously at her.

'We want somebody to put the arguments to them.'

'How . . . ?'

'By approaching them.'

'What do you mean? Go into the siege?'

'You know these boys, Mrs Cross. We know them too, we feel. Brown has a long record. We know they are not desperate criminals. They've been foolish boys and we intend to treat them as such, but of course you realise that our prime duty is to the hostages. Other people have volunteered to negotiate. Mostly Black Power maniacs and we don't want to put them in touch with anybody who'll make the situation worse.'

There was a silence and Burgess drew a long breath.

'I must be honest with you, Mrs Cross, and admit we've made a mistake in the way we've handled this siege.'

'I don't know what I can do.'

'I'll tell you. We've let it be known that the Greek man whom the boys released is dead. In fact he's not.'

'But I saw it in the papers! You're going to charge them with murder or manslaughter or whatever it is.'

'I'm letting you into a secret. I miscalculated. I take the blame. We hoped they would let the boy go, but they haven't. Let me be frank with you. We wanted to create the atmosphere for the release of the second hostage. We stand more of a chance against the three if they're holding only two adults.'

'You mean you're going to shoot them?'

'I'm afraid if they don't surrender very soon, we're going to have to take some strong steps. But before that, we want you to approach them. We want you to ask them to surrender and say that we'll see that it's taken into account at any trial that may follow.'

'What do I tell them about the man, about Mr Photopoulos?'

'Tell them the truth, tell them that the police have lied about him. They should be relieved. God knows what they've done to the little boy, his voice isn't coming through any of the devices.'

'You've bugged the place?'

'It'll contribute to your safety. We'll know exactly what's being said in the room and we'll intervene if

146

necessary. 'We've considered it all before asking you, Mrs Cross,' he added, 'and we've come to the conclusion that you'll be in no personal danger. The gunmen expect to have a pow-wow with someone. They've been asking us for one.'

'I don't think they'll listen to me at all,' faltered Edwina. 'You don't know Kwate . . . I mean Aloysius Brown.'

'We perhaps know him better than you think.'

Nineteen

'It has nothing to do with you,' Michael said when Edwina got back to the flat. 'Unless you think it has.'

'They just want me to pass a message.'

'I met the guy from BRAG – you know, the Black Revolutionary whatever-they-call-it. He's convinced that the police want a shoot-out. I don't think you ought to venture into that. Look what they did to the IRA thing, just walked in and killed two people.'

'It's not like that. I know these boys,' Edwina said. 'Those BRAG people are just maniacs. I think the police are playing it straight.'

'I never thought I'd hear you say *that*,' Michael said. 'They don't set a thief to catch a thief any more, it's all sociologists.'

Edwina wasn't concentrating on his words. She was thinking of the song that had gone round and round in her head in Kwate's room. Yes, she had smoked too much, she had had the drink he gave her, but everything, all the thrill she had felt, was not the product of wantonness. That's what Michael would have her feel. He was slowly, ever so gently, making her apologise. She should never have loved Rupert. Yes, loved him. She should try and live in a more sensible world. The song came back to her :

> *Come away, Miranda, day is done*
> *Night spreads its wings to follow the sun*

Come away, come away, come away
Time and the bell have buried the day.
Edwina phoned Burgess. 'I'll do it,' she said.
'Wear a tight-fitting sweater or shirt and come down
to the siege headquarters,' was the reply.

It was a small room on the ground floor of a building
fifty yards from the scene of the siege. Edwina was
fetched from her flat by P.C. Bully and a police driver.
'We saw your photographs,' Bully said. 'Very nice,
Mrs Cross. Very nice.'
His remark startled her.
'You've got Slingo?' she asked.
'Oh yes, we've got him. It was funny. He crashed into
a lamp-post a couple of miles from the place on the first
day. We didn't know what we'd got hold of till the next
day.'
'He gave you my name, did he?'
'As a matter of fact, he didn't. He wouldn't give us
anything. He pretended to be a drunken driver without
a licence. The constables at West Central took him for
just that. We found you through your photographs, Mrs
Cross. We looked all over the Brixton brothels, and
wasted about three days doing that. You school-teachers
shouldn't get involved in things like this, you know.'
At the siege headquarters Edwina was shown six
newspaper cuttings clipped onto a board. Burgess came
in as she studied them.
'I'm very glad you've agreed to co-operate, Mrs Cross.
We want you to absorb these facts. Here they are in
black and white.'
'I don't trust black or white.'
Burgess smiled. 'In print, I mean. Read this statement

from the Black Revolutionary Action Group; I believe you know of them.'

Edwina read the clipping. *The misguided youth are doing untold harm to community relations in this country. We must tell them that this isn't Trench Town. It's London. They are in the heart of the Capitalist Metropolis . . .'*

'You see, they don't want to know,' Burgess said. 'Then there's this,' he added, turning the page. 'See for yourself.'

Edwina read : *We call on the Home Secretary to take into account the repressive police action which has led to these tragic events.*

'That's some of our friends down in Brixton.'

'How do I know you didn't plant these?' Edwina asked. 'You'vé done very well with the television.'

'We have no control over these fly-by-night organisations, Mrs Cross. Also, look at this. The Cypriot community newspapers have appealed for the release of the boy Panos. We want you to tell them that.'

'But you told me his father's alive.'

'That's no reason for not releasing him. Mrs Cross, you are a brave woman. Play it by ear. We'll give you about half an hour. You've come in at their request, remember.'

'They asked for me?'

'Of course they did. We believe that a difference has arisen between Aloysius Brown and the other two, perhaps you could report on that.'

'I'm not reporting on anything, Mr Burgess. I'm simply going in there because my concern for life, I'm sure, is . . . er . . . deeper than yours.'

'No doubt.' Burgess smiled his cold smile.

He escorted her to the door with two other constables.

The path through the crowd and the reporters was cleared by the policemen standing around. She recalled her last words to Michael:

'Do you think they can really stop the papers from getting the story? Everyone knows we ran the drama group.'

He was watching her clean her face in the mirror and comb her wavy hair.

'Why do you insist on tarting yourself up?'

'I want to look as I normally do,' she had said, turning from the mirror.

'You'll be remembered as the girl who ended the mini-cab siege.'

'As the one who started it, maybe.'

'Or as the woman who sent the blacks to jail.'

Edwina wanted to tell him that if that was true, it would be because of him. She had decided to nail all this, all the events of the past six months, into a tidy coffin. He must help her. It was best that it ended this way. She could always pretend she was in charge till the end. People only blamed you for what you left unfinished and this was a way of finishing with the world she had flirted with.

Michael was strange. At the last minute, just before she left on her mission, he said, 'You're pleading with them to go to jail, you know that.'

'Maybe they deserve to go. And otherwise they'll be dead.'

'I don't understand you. Three weeks ago you'd have been singing hymns to black vitality.'

'Vitality has to make its terms with reality. Whatever you think, Michael, I don't think Rupert knows what he's got himself into.'

'Aw, poor little fellow, he just wanted to play Cowboy with the Great White Squaw.'

'You're so cynical.'

'No, I don't mean that. I say, that sweater looks quite good on you.'

She made a face at him as she left the room and went down to the waiting police car.

There are a thousand eyes watching her as she walks. Burgess says, 'No photographs, please, gentlemen.'

He has the loud-hailer in his hand. He raises it to the window.

'Kwate, a friend is coming to see you. Now.'

She hears Kwate's voice call back, 'Send him in.'

Edwina wipes her sweaty hands on the hips of her jeans. She is in the building. There are men in the room downstairs and two on the stairs as she passes. They nod to her.

She can't remember what she has been asked to say. She gets to the top of the stairs. There is no one there, just a tatty corridor leading to a door. She walks down it, her heart thumping furiously.

She doesn't know whether to knock on the door or to wait. As she hesitates, it opens. They have heard her coming. The first thing she sees is the muzzle of a pistol and she freezes. The door opens wider.

She desperately wants to go to the toilet. Her bladder is bursting, her guts rumble.

Kwate says, 'It's you.'

As she walks into the room, Edwina can see that Rupert is amazed. He is pleased that it's her.

'There are men in the corridor and in the alley at the back,' she says.

'They have gun?' Hurly asks.

Edwina expected a warmer reception. 'I think they have,' she says.

'OK, what you want?' Kwate asks. He is standing in the middle of the room, the shotgun over his shoulder. The hostages sit in a row at the edge of the settee. Rupert stands by the window, Hurly by the kitchen door. All three have their pistols and guns at the ready.

'I thought you wanted to talk to me. I haven't volunteered you know.' She looked at the boy. 'I have something to tell you. Can I sit down?'

Rupert motions her to the stool with his gun.

'The man Photopoulos is alive. He isn't dead. The police were trying some tricks on you.'

'You come here to take us?' Kwate asks. 'How come po-lis tell *you*. You give some police a little bit?'

'Talk to her straight, you,' Rupert shouts. 'Don't you see she's our last chance. I think she's telling the truth.'

'Have they got Slingo?' Hurly asks.

'They got him the first day. It's true. He crashed the car into a lamp-post.'

Hurly is the one who smiles.

'How did they get hold of you? They raid my house?' Rupert asks. Edwina doesn't answer the question.

'I didn't ask to see no white people,' Kwate states, and turns his back on her. 'She working for the police,' he says.

'I'm not working for anyone. They told me you wanted to say something and they wanted you to know that the murder . . . the death of this boy's – '

'Murder! We didn't touch nobody. You ask these people. You come in here and start calling – '

Kwate is interrupted by Rupert. 'Let her talk.'

'She's your girl,' Kwate says. 'You let her talk. I don't want no white chick negotiating for me.'

'What shall I tell them?' Edwina asks Rupert.

'Don't know.'

'They want you to release the boy. I think the police are serious about shooting it out.'

'The boy ain't leaving here,' Kwate says. 'If anyone else want to leave, they could leave, but I'll deal with them.' He moves to the kitchen door and raises the shotgun.

'Listen,' Edwina says to him. 'The police showed me cuttings from the black revolutionary groups, and they don't support you.'

'You can't trust that woman, she tells too much lie,' Kwate says.

'It's you who tell the lies,' Edwina shouts back. 'I'm not scared of your little rifle, Kwate. I've come to try and help, and if it freaks you out to hear what's going on, well, you'll have to take it.'

'No, look,' Rupert says. 'There's only one way out of here. If we can get to the Jamaican embassy, we're safe aren't we? They could fly us out.'

'I don't think there's much hope of that, but I'll say what you want me to say.' Edwina hadn't expected this sort of confusion. She'd imagined she'd give them a message, they'd put their demands, she'd be free.

'This woman working with the pigs,' Kwate says. 'She's come to freak us out.'

'Is Slingo working with the police?' Rupert asks.

'I don't know anything about that. I was talking to Bully on the way here. He said that Slingo didn't tell them anything. They didn't even know he was with you.'

'How they find you then?' Hurly asks.

Edwina avoids the question again. She shoots a glance at Rupert. 'I'll tell you what I think, if you want to know. The place is absolutely surrounded by police. I

can't see that you'll ever get away.' She turns to Rupert.
'I've talked to Michael about this too. You respect his
opinion, don't you? He thinks – '

'Don't try and play games with boy, woman,' Kwate
interrupts.

'It's you who are playing the games, Kwate. You've
got them into this mess. Look at these people. They don't
even know what you're arguing about. You'd use anybody, just to prove that you're the fastest mouth in the
West. You might want to prove that you're a martyr.
You're posing as a great revolutionary, but everyone
outside, at least, knows what you are, a petty hustler
and a small time thief. I don't care if you don't want to
use me as go-between, but these people have a say in it,
too. You're playing with their lives.'

'I'll use you when I want,' Kwate replies. 'I know how
you play. It's kicks for you and bullets for us. It's my
life you messing with.'

'It's everybody's life, Kwate,' Rupert says.

'They send in their wooden horse,' Hurly says, his
eyes distant. He doesn't seem to be participating in the
argument. He has slouched back on the settee, and is
pointing the gun towards himself, shutting one eye and
looking down the barrel.

Everyone in the room turns to him.

'What you think, Hurly,' Kwate shouts.

Hurly smiles at all of them. 'You deal with it, guv.
This woman is your woman and she Rupert woman and
she everybody woman, and you say she police woman,
so don't ask me. I don't have no woman.'

Kwate looks alarmed. 'Look, she freak the man out.
Get the bitch out of here!' He goes swiftly up to Hurly
and grabs the pistol from his hand. Hurly lets go of the
pistol and begins to laugh on the settee.

'They send horse into the citadel, and the hoss graze in all pastures.'

'Get out of here,' Kwate commands.

Edwina gets up. The hostages sit transfixed. Hurly chuckles to himself, and looking at him, Kwate's blood seems to drain out of his face. He motions to Rupert to take Edwina out.

Rupert has his revolver in her back as she goes into the corridor. She takes four or five steps and an impulse grabs her. She turns round.

'Rupert, I may not see you again. Please listen to reason.'

'Keep moving,' Rupert says, menacingly, holding out his revolver.

She turns round again and starts towards the stairs.

'You thought it was Slingo,' she says. 'But it wasn't. It was that madman in there. I know what he's after. He got you into this, now you get yourself out of it. I've done what I can.'

Suddenly he is upon her. She feels herself grabbed by the neck of the sweater.

'All right, bitch, just keep walking. You're taking me out of here. I'm going to get out of here.' His voice falters, but she feels his breath, and his grip is firm, pushing her down the stairs.

'Don't make no move, or I'll kill her. I don't care if you kill me,' Rupert says to the two men in the downstairs room who jump aside as he forces her to the door, blindly, firmly.

'Rupert, don't! Let me go,' Edwina shouts. But she feels the determination in his grip, and the kick of his knee as he moves her on, almost lifting her off her feet.

He pushes her to the door. There is a cry from the crowd as the two figures come into sight.

'That way,' she hears him whisper, hoarsely, forcing her to the side of the door.

'*Rupert!*' There is a loud scream from the first floor window. Edwina thinks she recognises Hurly's voice, and then two or three or four or five shots ring out. Rupert falls against her as though he has stumbled, as though he's collided with her while running, and she sees the pavement come up and hit her face, and, in an instant of blankness and terror, there are hands all around her.

'Get her out of the way.'

She is dragged by two men along the pavement, close to the wall and the gunfire explodes, *toph, toph, toph,* all around her, seeming to her to boom in the distance.

Twenty

Hurly remembers a boy bewildered by the task of arriving at the truth, the truth that lawyers wanted to know, the truth that friends nagged him for, the truth that was to be presented to a jury and the truth that was going to come back to him again and again as a vision of something he had done, something he must remember himself as doing. What might have happened was mixed up with what actually happened.

Kwate was at the window. He told them that. Kwate was led out of the room by five men who held his arms while he himself held his own stomach, the blood crawling over his hands.

He remembers the shout that escaped him, the hope and despair that were wrung from his throat and lungs. 'Rupert!' he'd shouted. 'Rupert!' He remembers the certainty that Rupert was dead; he didn't need to be told. He was gone as certainly as his hope of vaulting the walls of Babylon; the Babylon that surrounded his body, surrounded his spirit, turned all longing into waiting.

Hurly remembers a boy who made no plans because plans were for tomorrow and today was more important. Kwate had shed tears as he was led out of the doorway. He remembers the clear vision, the instant feeling of being able to hold for ever in his mind every little detail of what he saw, what he heard. Kwate's feet had gone limp with pain as they dragged him through the door. The girl and the white man and the boy had left before them, walking out of the room like people who were first in a queue. Hurly remembers standing up, the terror of the ten pistols that pointed at him, he remembers raising his arms and resting them behind his head. He was no longer part of Kwate's plan, now that he could look into tomorrow, into the day after.

The people crowded into the gallery of the court. They were still the audience, but he was no longer an actor. They gave him fist salutes. He made them a speech which he rehearsed with his lawyer in the grey cell below the courtroom. He remembers the feeling of being beyond judgement, beyond wanting to dodge, with evidence and cunning, the fact of what he had done, the fact of what must be done. The newspapers published his statements. A black man and a black woman came to see him in Brixton prison. They told him he should say that he didn't recognise the court. He asked them if he should say he didn't recognise the handcuffs. They brought him cuttings from the papers. He kept them for a few weeks and then flushed them down the toilet.

His cell-mate, who talks of 'tie-up men' and 'bird' and 'porridge', counts the weeks as workers at the end of a working day count the minutes. He talks to his cell-mate about 'survival', a word he must never forget. It's more than a day's job, this 'survival', more than the decision to be the way you want to be. It's other people, what they want of you, how you fit into their world, how they darken your rainbow by clouding your sky.

He remembers every word of the books he reads. The Greek man comes to see him on Saturdays. The girl visits him now on Saturdays and Sundays. She brings him some books; she wants the boy to forget. She talks about tomorrow and he never reminds her that tomorrow drags along its yesterday; it goes forward like a wounded animal dragging a trap. She talks of the new jobs she has, she talks to him of the trades he could learn, she tries to tell him that to make peace with Babylon he will have to forget.

But Hurly doesn't want to forget, he wants to remember.